Best Friends Forever

L. MOONE

CONTENTS

CHAPTER ONE

* Jill *

What started as any other day, shooting a popular cooking show at Pinewood Studios in Iver Heath, has turned into an impromptu crew meeting. This is going to suck. The news that our executive producer, Claire, plans to announce couldn't be any worse.

I've just finished rounding everyone up, when Claire begins her announcement.

"Guys! You might have been wondering why we went off schedule today and where I've been all afternoon." She pauses to allow the swell of chatter to die down around us. "The rumors are true. It was nice while it lasted, but I'm sorry to announce that *Decadent Desserts* is no more."

The tension is palpable, and as a result, I can feel a nervous giggle getting stuck somewhere halfway up my throat. *Not now, dammit!*

I glance around the crowd of two dozen fellow crew members to distract myself as well as figure out what everyone must be thinking. Some look surprised, others, not so much. One girl—Nicole, who does the make-up—has a smug smirk on her face. Weird. For all she knows, she's about to lose her job along with the rest of us.

Finally, my eyes land on Damien—my favorite person in the world—and I relax. Although he's the tallest guy in the room by far, he's doing his best to blend in. Of course he fails. Hard as he may try, he'll never be just one of the crowd.

Our eyes meet for just a second, and the corner of my mouth starts to twitch with the beginnings of a smile. A smile is still better than actually laughing out loud like I normally would at the worst possible time. Considering the gravity of what Claire has just announced, it would just be misinterpreted.

I warned Damien earlier that something big was going to happen today, to ensure he wouldn't be taken by surprise. He guessed the details from there. So now he's looking at me already in support, during what he knows is a stressful situation for me.

We look out for each other like that. That's what best friends do. Short of secret handshakes or matching bracelets, that's exactly what we are and have been, ever since we started interning together a couple of years ago. Looking at how comfortable we are around each other, you'd think we've known each other forever, and not just since college.

Once the rest of the crew calms down, Claire carries on. "I want to make it very clear that I don't blame anyone here, and neither does the network. We delivered excellent work on the previous season, and this season was on track to become a winner as well. Byron's career has run its course, in part due to his own attitude and behavior, and in part—well, I don't need to tell you what was *really* going on here. The full story will hit the tabloids soon enough, so you can all read up on it in your own time. The big news for us is that the network will launch Ethan to fill Byron's time slot after rebranding. I'm sure I speak for everyone here that we wish him all the best, because he truly deserves it."

A murmur travels around the crowd. Many of my colleagues nod solemnly.

Although it was supposed to be Byron Ainsworth who was the star of *Decadent Desserts,* nobody liked him. *No one.* He won't be missed. Claire is right. Ethan earned his big break. It helps that the mouthwatering recipes featured on the show were his all along.

"So, what's the timeline for the rebrand?" our director of photography, Gavin, pipes up.

Claire clicks her tongue. "That's the catch. It could be a few months. It depends on what the suits decide. In any case, I won't be around for that project. Craig will be back from paternity leave by then, so he'll handle it. I've informed him of the change already."

"Are they changing the whole look: everything?" Stevie, the set designer, asks.

Claire nods. "They want to give Ethan a fresh start, so yes, there will be a completely new set. The exact direction for the new show hasn't been decided yet, but I'm sure Craig will reach out to you once he gets more details."

I exhale sharply. Tough crowd. But then, Claire knows how to handle these things. I'm glad she briefed me in advance, or I would've freaked out by now. It's a tough gig, being an executive producer. I don't know how she makes it look so easy. Maybe one day I'll be as chill as she is.

"Unfortunately, that means that for now, all our contracts stand cancelled. We simply don't have a show to shoot anymore."

Now the news has hit home. The intensity of the whispers around the room has swelled again.

"But—" Claire raises her voice in an attempt to get everyone's attention again. "There is a tiny little silver lining! While the rebrand takes place, I've been given a small budget to sign a few of you on for a reality show…"

"Fucking hate reality TV," Gavin complains. "The hours are too long."

"The hours won't be too bad, as it's going to be shot episodically," Claire says.

"How many of us?" one of the post-production team, Susan, asks.

"The contract is only for a short six-episode

season to test the waters, so it's going to be a small budget and hence a tight crew. We'll wrap it up within a couple of months, and then we'll see." Claire turns to me and points at the sheet of paper in my hand.

My heart is racing now. It's my last chance to get what I want. I glance at the short-listed names Claire had given me earlier and lean in close enough to have a word with her.

"Hey, I really do think you're going to need someone else on camera," I whisper. "No matter how compelling the material is, if the camera work is too basic, we'll never get renewed for a second season."

She stares at me for a second, then nods. "Fine. Damien is in. But that means I won't have the finances to hire help for you. So…?"

"I'll do it all. Just make sure you get Damien," I urge her. "You'll thank me later."

Claire straightens herself. "Gavin, if you'd do me the honor?"

"No odd hours or complex locations?" he asks.

"Promise. Single location. Fixed camera angles. Regular schedule. No funny business."

"Done."

"And your man, Damien," she says.

Gavin shrugs and folds his arms. Sweet relief. I knew I could get my way with Claire, so the only remaining kink in my plan was Gavin, who could have vetoed Claire's request.

I keep my eyes trained on Damien, who meets my gaze across the room and smiles. Yep, he's realized that I made this happen. After everything he's been telling me about saving up to move out of his cramped house share, I simply had to. And even otherwise. I'm friendly with the entire crew, but things between Damien and I are at another level. I live for the little breaks we spend together every day. The chit chat about pop culture, life, or even the weather and the chance to just be myself with another person who would never judge me for it.

"Luke on sound. Stevie, I'd like you to be in charge of the set. Susan and Kate, I need you for post-production and story development. Nicole will be doing the make-up, and last but not least, Jill, will be my ever-present eyes and ears and fill in anywhere else." Claire turns to me and winks.

I know she means it. *Anywhere else.* Fine. As long as Damien is on the crew, I'll do it. I'll do the recruiting. The babysitting of contestants. The paperwork. Talking people down when they're inevitably having a meltdown. Fetching refreshments.*Anything.*

"I wish I had better news for the rest of you. Hopefully the rebrand will happen quickly and you can all sign on with Craig for Ethan's new show eventually."

Claire clears her throat again. "Guys, everyone! We've got until tomorrow evening to pack up the set and clear out. Let's do what we can today and grab a few drinks tonight as sort of a farewell before finishing up in the morning."

Most everyone murmurs in agreement before going about their business. Come rain or shine, great ratings or cancellations, the show must go on. The more seasoned members of the crew are used to the drill by now. Some might even be glad to get the time off.

Soon enough, only Claire's new skeleton crew is left standing in a semi-circle around her.

"What's the concept?" Luke asks. "It's not a bloody talent show, is it? Because in that case I'd need extra resources."

"It's a dating show. Nothing you couldn't manage in your sleep," Claire says.

Luke just shrugs. Gavin and Stevie have also got their poker faces firmly on.

Now that Damien is on the team, I'm getting more and more excited, though. Dating reality shows are my guilty pleasure. The long hours we tend to work don't leave much time for vegging out in front of the TV, so it'll be good fun helping create one.

And a tiny little part of me is wondering if following around a bunch of singles actively trying to find love is going to invite Cupid back into my own life. I hope so. I've been single for a couple of years now; it's well beyond time for a change.

"Well, this is all I've got for the moment. Expect a call from me soon. Meanwhile, let's get back to it!" Claire says, ending the meeting.

Damien takes a position right next to me and gently bumps into my shoulder. This brief contact between us makes me feel warm and fuzzy inside. "Thanks for putting in a good word, hey!"

I smile awkwardly. "Don't mention it. You would have done the same thing."

"What was the catch? Don't think I didn't notice the little negotiation between you and Claire."

"Ah, it's no big deal." Only my very own assistant. A chance to outsource all the irritating menial tasks that need doing for a show like this in favor of taking on more responsibility in influencing the actual creative direction. It's a worthwhile trade-off, though. I love having someone on set who will always be on my side.

"Liar," he says.

"Fine. Claire was going to hire another assistant."

Damien scoffs. "Cutting down on cinematics in favor of an extra production assistant would have been a bad call."

I smile briefly. Only a camera operator would say that with so much conviction.

"That's what I told her. It's all in the interest of the show," I say, the cheer in my voice sounding a bit more forced now. I wish we could just skip past this conversation. I did a thing. No need to make a big deal about it.

He stares at me a little longer than normal, making things even more awkward. I don't even know why I'm uneasy about it. Damien is the sweetest person I know. But right now, a certain weirdness hangs in the air which I can't wait to get rid of.

"I'd better get to work now like Claire said. You'll come to the pub later?" I change the topic.

"Wouldn't miss it!"

A quick smile and nod later, I leave him standing there and leg it after Claire, who is already heading for the editing room. We've got a lot of work to do before we can even think of getting out of here.

She pauses and turns towards me just before she opens the door. "Jill, see if you can get a hold of Ethan. He's been such a good sport throughout, it would be rude not to ask if he wants to come along in the evening. And we'll also have to get his stuff out of here by tomorrow, so make the necessary arrangements with him."

"Sure thing." I turn on my heels and head straight for the prep kitchen that has been Ethan's domain up until now. I wonder what must be going through his head. The big break the network is planning for him couldn't have happened to a nicer, more deserving guy. And his cooking. *Oh. My. God.* The entire crew had figured out an age ago that Byron was just a bag of hot air and Ethan was the real deal.

I knock on the door, more as a formality than anything else, but predictably the prep kitchen is dark and abandoned. Of course he's not here; he found out about the cancellation before anyone else, I'm sure. Duh!

After taking a quick look around, mentally assessing how long it'll take to pack up all the equipment and supplies, I fish my phone out of my pocket and dial his number.

It takes a while, but he picks up eventually.

"Hey, Ethan?" I say. "Claire asked me to call you. Congratulations, first of all!"

He mumbles his thanks, but it's obvious that he feels awkward about it. I'm about to go into pep-talk mode, when I remember that that isn't really my job anymore. Plus, he's got plenty of time to let the news sink in, so I pivot to the real reason for my call.

"Actually, I'm supposed to arrange for your stuff to be packed up. If you can text me your address, I'll have it delivered to you tomorrow," I say. "And also, we're all wondering if you'd like to join the crew for farewell drinks tonight…"

He is quick to agree. Claire was right to include him. He might be on the verge of a major career upgrade, but for the time being, he's still just one of the crew. It'll be nice to be able to congratulate him in person tonight.

CHAPTER TWO

*** Damien ***

Okay, that was weird. Not that Jill got me onto Claire's team, that was quite… Well, she was right. I would have done the same for her, except nobody ever asks the junior camera operator if he has any recommendations for assistant producers. That's just not how these things work.

But her reaction when I tried to thank her was odd. Awkward. Like she was regretting it a little.

It's been a confusing few months. Ever since Claire took over the *Decadent Desserts* set from Craig, Jill has cemented her position as Claire's number two, and they have become nearly inseparable. Good for her. She's earned it through hard work and complete dedication. Jill is the sort of person who always goes the extra mile.

We might have started as interns at the same time after graduating in Film & TV Production together. But Jill's career is making quick upward progress, and mine seems to have stagnated for now. Not that that's necessarily a problem. I love my work, most of the time. And Gavin has recently started giving me more autonomy as well as occasional mentoring sessions to develop my very own cinematic style, so I guess he thinks I have some potential too.

I just… Jill is such a bright star who can infect an entire set with her enthusiasm and passion for her work. Not in an obnoxious, crass way, but with quiet persistence. I really admire that, along with so many other things I admire about her.

But how long will it take before Jill outgrows our friendship? Before she moves on to bigger, better things and can no longer orchestrate a way for me to tag along wherever she goes. Or maybe she'll no longer even want to be stuck with me. Because everything she is, I am not. I'm not an optimist. I'm not chatty and sociable and comfortable around a lot of people like she is. I'm like a great big geeky anchor: happy to stay behind the camera, but also keeping her from soaring on her own.

It's that possibility that's been in the back of my mind for a while now, but more so today.

She didn't spell it out, but I immediately understood that she would have been in charge of the other assistant Claire wanted. It would have meant a promotion. No more fetching coffees or lunches or any of the other stuff junior production assistants usually get saddled with. But she chose *me* instead. It's humbling. And panic-inducing.

How am I supposed to deal with that? How can I

ever repay her?

I'm lost in thought while dismantling the lights set-up towards the right side of the stage. As a result, I don't notice Gavin when he tries to talk to me.

A finger snap near my face finally forces me to focus on his presence.

"Oi! Where's your head at, Damien?" Gavin says.

"Sorry, boss. Thinking about the new show."

"Right." Gavin shrugs. "Claire better hope the format doesn't change, or I'll be outta there before she realizes."

He makes a show of cracking his back and neck and looks at me with a crooked smile on his face. "If it's going to be a bunch of horny kids who think sleeping around on TV is going to make them famous, and I'm expected to run after them with my camera at all hours of the night... I'm getting too old for that *shite*, you hear me?"

"Yep. I hear you," I mumble. Is that what he thinks the show is going to be? Ugh, I hope not! The last thing I need is to spend the next couple of months observing orgies through my camera lens. Painfully close to the action and yet impossibly far away. Jesus, I'm turning into a cynical bastard just like him!

"Get this stuff packed up neatly, alright? I don't want to have to untangle even a single wire later," Gavin says.

"Got it. This isn't my first day on the job. Plus, you'd just make me redo it anyway if I get it wrong."

"Don't you know it! Carry on."

As soon as Gavin leaves me to it, I do what I always do on set: I pretend to be fully absorbed in my work, while actually keeping an eye out for Jill in my peripheral vision. Once I spot her coming out of the prep kitchen, it immediately makes me feel better, sort of.

How does it matter what the new show is going to be about? As long as *she'll* be there, it'll be bearable. And despite my earlier reservations about her career, she did choose to bring me onboard, at least this time.

The last thing I should be doing right now is letting my own lack of a love life get me down. I ought to be more proactive; that's what I should do. Maybe reactivate my profiles and give internet dating another shot. Who knows, watching a bunch of other people go on first dates might teach me a thing or two.

But then… Dating. *Ugh.*

The only person I want to be dating is standing right there, talking enthusiastically with her phone pressed up to her ear. *Jill.*

Beautiful, intelligent, ambitious, talented Jill. The whole package. My soul mate, though she'll never know it, because I sure as hell am not going to tell her.

BEST FRIENDS FOREVER

I've seen her type when it comes to men, and I'm basically the exact opposite. Through our shared love for superhero movies, I've learned that her celebrity crush is Chris Hemsworth as *Thor*. The antithesis of me personified, unless you count fat Thor from *Endgame*, and even then.

Anyway, nobody counts fat Thor from *Endgame*.

Her crush on regular-sized Thor tracks perfectly with the guy she used to date when we were still in college. Frank-something, an aspiring actor with perfect blond hair and confidence—almost cockiness—and a gym bod to match.

No, Jill and I are friends, but that's it. It's the best I can hope for.

That's not so bad, is it?

* Jill *

Time flies when you're wrapping up a project. Before I know it, it's time to head to the pub with the rest of the crew. Since there's no local public transport to speak of, I catch a ride with Stevie, who somehow always ends up being the designated driver for a handful of us whenever we go out as a group.

Nicole joins us too, as well as Damien, who automatically gets the passenger seat. There's no way he could fold his large frame into the back of Stevie's slightly tired VW Beetle, anyway.

"Weird, huh? We should have been shooting the second half of the season next week. Instead…" My eyes settle on Damien's back while I speak.

He's so damn tall, his shoulders stick out above the seat, and he's hunching over a little. The sight of him sitting in this silly little car always manages to tickle me.

"That's just life, isn't it? All Byron had to do was carry on playing his role with at least an ounce of humility, but instead he ruined it for everyone, including himself," Stevie grumbles.

Nicole doesn't say anything, she just stares out the window with a subtle smile playing on her lips. It's a nice view: the English countryside lit up by the bright summer sun. Still, her demeanor puzzles me.

"You're awfully quiet, Nicole," I tell her.

"I'm content. There's nothing awful about it," she responds.

Yeah, right.

"I can't help but be curious…" Damien says.

"About?" I ask.

"What Claire said about Byron's behavior. I mean, we all know he was a douche, but these newly famous types generally are. I wonder what he actually *did* that got him fired from his own show. Unless someone complained formally, how would the network even find out about what he was like on set? And surely, no one on the crew…"

That question had occurred to me too, but it seemed too delicate to bring up directly.

Nicole shifts uncomfortably next to me, but she keeps her eyes fixed on the lush green landscape and bright blue skies outside.

"Even if someone did complain, that's always confidential, and for good reason. We may never know what happened," I say, observing Nicole from the corner of my eye. *Confidential* it might have been, but the identity of the complainant is no longer a secret in my opinion.

"Hey, have I mentionedthat Ethan is also coming to the pub?" I say.

"Nice! I didn't think I'd get the chance to congratulate him properly," Damien says.

"Yeah. It was Claire's idea."

"Couldn't have happened to a nicer guy," Stevie remarks, while flipping on the turn signal and slowing down for the turn leading to the pub. "I hope he brought dessert."

I lean back in my seat and close my eyes while remembering Ethan's various creations on set. Spectacular, every single one. My stomach growls painfully in response.

Stevie parks in the first available spot and all of us spill out of her tiny car and head for the entrance to the rustic-looking country inn. This is exactly the sort of thing that makes shoots at Pinewood so enjoyable.

The rural setting, with all its perks, all within relatively easy reach of London. Since we don't know yet where the next project will take us, this could be our farewell from Pinewood as well.

After entering the establishment, we make our way towards the back where the event rooms are. The many framed photos on the wall along the hallway reveal that this pub has a long history of hosting film and TV crews a lot more famous than we are. The list of celebrities who have visited this place over the years is staggering. I love studying the many pictures whenever we come in. Every time I spot a new famous face.

Damien joins me and points at an old black and white shot. "Ha. Sean Connery looks so young in that one."

"I guess that must have been from when they shot *Dr. No*," I speculate.

Stevie opens the door to the room we'd reserved for the occasion, inspiring a roar of excitement from the people already inside. It's a full house tonight. Claire's idea of treating this as a farewell party inspired even the more unsociable members of the crew to turn up.

"Wow, okay, I guess we're late and they're already sloshed," Damien remarks, running his hand across the five-o-clock-shadow on his chin.

I grin up at him. "In that case, we have some

catching up to do."

"Let's do it." He offers me his arm and we cross the rest of the hallway together. I love it when he does little stuff like this. Such a gentleman.

Once inside, upon seeing the pitchers of beer and cider that await us on the long wooden table that graces the center of the room, it doesn't take long for everyone to be swept up in the festivities.

As per usual, whenever alcohol flows, so do the stories. I find a seat across from Claire, who is already in conversation with Ethan by the time I get my glass filled up.

"Sarah didn't come?" I overhear Claire ask, a knowing grin on her face.

I frown. Why would Sarah—a journalist we only met for the first time last week—be invited to a crew party?

"Oh, she had to be back at the office today," Ethan explains. "Her article is going live this weekend."

I stare at Ethan for a moment, then at Claire, who winks at me. The penny starts to drop. Oh, damn! Ethan and Sarah! In hindsight, it makes perfect sense. They did spend a lot of time together this past week.

"Congratulations again, Ethan," I interject. "We're all super excited to see what the rebrand will bring. And to try some new recipes, of course!"

He nods and smiles into his drink. "Thanks, Jill."

"It'll be amazing," Claire says. "And Craig is exactly the right guy to give you a leg up. *Decadent Desserts* was his baby from the start, anyway. Before his wife had an actual baby."

"I remember him from last season," Ethan says.

I'm quick to nod in agreement.

"You guys won't be on the crew?" Ethan asks.

I wait for Claire to answer first. "Ah, I was offered my own little project, actually. A reality show. Full creative control. Jill will be helping me."

"If that doesn't deserve a toast, I don't know what does!" Ethan says, raising his glass.

"It's a pretty big deal, actually," I agree, raising my own drink in response.

"Hey, Ethan! Congrats!" Damien sits down beside me and leans in closer. "What else are we toasting?"

"The new show we're doing," I tell him, glancing up at his kind face. His presence never fails to make me feel at ease.

"Ah yes, to our new show!" Damien agrees. "We should get some shots to celebrate."

"You too?" Ethan asks him. "You're all moving on?"

"It's only a short contract; a couple of months tops. After that, who knows? Some of us might end up working together again in future," Claire tells him. "Ours is a small world."

Damien gets up for a moment to place our drinks

order, then sits back down next to me.

"Hey, do you guys remember when we just started recording the first season, that time the whipped cream can exploded in Byron's face?" Damien says.

We share a laugh. "That was classic. Can't we convince the network to release a blooper reel? We've got hours of amazing footage like that, just going to waste," I say.

Claire presses her lips together, pretending to be the serious one. I know better than to take her stoic expression at face value. "Isn't his public fall from grace thanks to Sarah's upcoming article already bad enough?" she asks.

"Could still be funny," Damien remarks.

"I'd watch it," Stevie enters the conversation while sitting down at the head of the table.

A waitress arrives with a tray full of shots, and Damien distributes them among us. "Bottoms up!"

We each pick up our drink and down it in one gulp. My god, it's strong.

"What on earth did you order?" I whisper at him.

Damien just grins at me. It's funny, how his eyes sparkle in this light. Did he always have piercing blue eyes like this? How did I never notice before…

Ethan clears his throat and suppresses a smile. "Allow me to play devil's advocate for a moment here. Who knows, a few months down the line there'll be a crew a lot like this one, thinking about releasing bloopers from *my* upcoming show…"

Damien chuckles. "Ah, yes. You'd be a good sport about it though, wouldn't you?"

Ethan shrugs. "Perhaps, but hopefully I wouldn't have gotten cancelled already."

"Fair point. We shouldn't speak ill of the cancelled," I say.

"Actually," Nicole pipes up somewhere behind me. "The *cancelled* can go fuck himself."

Everyone around the table is speechless while exchanging wide-eyed stares. Nicole leans over the table, grabs one of the extra shots, and downs it.

"Wow," I mumble. "Tell us how you *really* feel!"

Stevie lets out a nervous chuckle.

"Seriously. The guy was a pig. Good fucking riddance," Nicole complains, picking up a second shot glass and drinking that in one go as well.

"Oookay," Claire says. "Anyone hungry?"

Those early drinks have gone straight to my head, so I'm quick to raise my hand.

"Probably should have eaten first," I mumble. And Nicole too, from the looks of her.

CHAPTER THREE

Except for the unpleasantness of Nicole's outburst, the *Decadent Desserts* farewell party is a grand success. Without a show to shoot early the next morning, everyone lets their hair down.

Alcohol flows freely and quite a few of us stay late. Come midnight, we're all a bit worse for wear, especially Jill. This surprises me a little. I don't think I've ever seen her party this hard.

Early in the evening, I was still wondering if she was overcompensating for the loss of that possible promotion. She didn't seem upset, though. Not even now that she's quite tipsy.

She spends most the evening laughing with the others, humming along to the music playing in the background, and resting her head on my shoulder whenever she sits down next to me. It's really rather sweet and makes it all the harder to keep myself under control.

Because when she gets that close, I want to do nothing more than to reach out and caress her hair, and bury my face in it.

She's so innocent. Her affections are friendly, whereas mine would cross an invisible line. You don't sniff your friends' hair. It's just not done.

God, I want to, though.

I also want to hold her hand. And ask her if she regrets choosing me over getting her very own assistant. I don't, obviously. It would only bring down the mood of a perfectly good party.

So instead of speaking my mind, I smile whenever she smiles at me. Laugh whenever anyone makes a joke. Participate in the obligatory leg-pulling and banter.

I try not to think about Jill's lips: soft and kissable and only inches away. Or her slender fingers, tapping the table along to some pop song that's started playing…

If this is as good as it gets—this friendship of ours—should I not savor this? The fact that she trusts me to be herself. To lean on me when she's tired, because she undoubtedly must be after the day we've all had. To share her worries for the upcoming show. She wonders whether she'll be able to wrangle a bunch of amateurs in case they get cold feet about dating on TV.

She'll be perfect, of course, which I assure her of.

That's what friends do. Which is what we are and always will be. And that has to be enough.

By the time the pub's wait staff tell us that it's

closing time, most of us are exhausted, even if everyone's still unwilling to admit it. It's been a long few weeks leading up to tonight.

Stevie—the sober one of the lot—dutifully gets up first. "Let's make a move, then!"

Everyone else groans and complains as they start to gather their belongings. Jill looks especially drowsy. If we stayed any longer, I'm pretty sure she'd end up dozing off in her chair.

Some of the others take out their phones and start organizing their rides home, which gives me an idea.

"Hey, Jill, how about we share a cab? That way Stevie doesn't have to go out of her way," I suggest.

Jill smiles sweetly and nods while suppressing a yawn. It kills me how adorable she looks right now. I try not to stare, and instead open Uber to get us a ride. Despite so many of us doing the same thing, there are plenty of cars to be found. Before long, all of us have booked one, and we start spilling onto the large terrace towards the front of the pub to wait.

Only then do I realize I've also been at it a bit too hard tonight. Still, my walk is significantly steadier than Jill's, who continues to lean on my arm all the way. It's a balmy summer's evening, so the pub terrace is not a bad place to spend a few minutes until our car arrives.

When it finally does, I get her settled on the backseat first before walking around to take a seat beside her. She's immediately cuddled up next to me with her head on my shoulder again. Her soft, smooth hair brushes against my cheek, and I barely know what to do with myself.

The car starts to move, and I close my eyes and try to steady my breathing. Two minutes into the drive, I can't stand it any longer and place my arm around her, which only makes her melt into me more. My heart races, and my breaths grow shallow. And I try my damnedest not to let it show.

She's just tired, I tell myself. This isn't the first or last time we've ended up driving home together. Having her this close to me is making me *want* things, though. Things I shouldn't want.

"So, Damien," she whispers, just loud enough for me to hear over the car stereo.

"Mhm?"

"We're friends, right?"

"Yup." Unfortunately *just* friends.

"Have you ever thought… What if?"

My throat closes up so tight, I can't even respond to that. Only every single day and every night.

"I mean… Some friends… They have, like, benefits," Jill mumbles.

My heart rate shoots through the roof. I close my eyes and focus on just breathing in and out. Jesus. She's drunk. She couldn't possibly mean it. Friends with benefits; *us?* Why? She's easily a nine, whereas

I'm more like a four. What's in it for her?

"So, like, what if…" Jill's voice trails off. I start to wonder if she's fallen asleep, when suddenly she starts to speak again. "This is nice, right?"

"Yup," I croak. It *is* nice, in an agonizingly painful way.

"We ought to be friends with cuddle benefits. You give the best hugs." She grabs my arm, tugs it tighter around her, and sighs.

Only now can I breathe a little again. Okay. Now it makes sense. Because she couldn't possibly be into me *like that*. Not Jill. I've seen the sort of guys she goes out with, and I'm so not it.

But yeah, as much as it hurts to think that this will never lead anywhere, Jill can cuddle with me any time she wants. I put my other arm around her and just sit there, in the back of our Uber, trying to ignore the seductive scent of her hair, the tempting warmth of her body, and the gaping hole in my heart where hope used to live.

This is it. This is the best it's going to get. If I can stop fixating on everything we'll never be, then this is pretty damn good.

But it still hurts. If I want it to stop, I'm going to have to make a few changes. Be more proactive. I can't put my love life on hold and expect that things are magically going to change. I know I'll love her forever, but we'll always be just friends. And if I want to appreciate that about us, I'd better try to find romance someplace else.

Jill

I reach the studio not-so-bright-nor-early the next morning. My head is still pounding after the excesses of last night. How did that even happen? Oh yeah, for a change the entire team came out to the pub, and predictably, things got out of hand. Everything went a bit wonky after the first round of shots.

I'm never drinking on an empty stomach again.

Luckily there isn't much to do today. I managed to pack up most of Ethan's gear already, so I just have to wait for the transport. And in the meantime, a few of us are going to help Stevie finish dismantling the set. That's it.

By the time I make it inside and finally dare to take off my sunglasses, it takes my eyes extra long to adjust to the dim lighting. Damien's already here and greets me with an amused grin on his face.

"Morning."

"Bleh," I respond.

"About last night…" he starts.

I smile back at him half-heartedly. Not because I feel like it, but because his presence just does that to me. He never fails to make me smile even when I feel crappy.

BEST FRIENDS FOREVER

Even though I would have loved nothing more than to stay under the covers all day and nurse this hangover. And relive a beautiful, sexy dream I had, so that I might remember more of what it was about or who was in it. Because all I have right now is just a lingering sense of loss for something that will never be. And a splitting headache.

"Yeah, not doing *that* ever again. Next time, stop me," I grumble.

He averts his gaze. "Things did go a bit far this time."

"They did." Why isn't he looking at me anymore? What'd I say? Did I do something wrong last night?

"Well, I think Stevie is already here and waiting, so we'd better get going," Damien says.

"'Kay."

He leaves abruptly, forcing me to almost jog behind him to keep up. One pace of his takes two of mine to cross. Stupid short legs.

Other than the rather comical size difference between us, we're normally quite perfect together. We like the same sorts of movies and share a sense of humor. Even our musical tastes overlap.

Perfect. Like best friends should be. So what's wrong right now?

A fuzzy memory of last night comes back to me and my heart twists painfully in response. Did that really happen, in the Uber home? It must have. And it would explain his weird behavior this morning.

Did I really utter the words "friends with benefits" in front of Damien last night? I remember him reacting like one of those fainting goats when they get startled by a loud noise. He just froze. *Of course he's being weird.* He probably remembers that bizarre conversation a lot more clearly than I do.

Crap.

I keep stealing glances at him while we help Stevie with the props and the set. Normally I often catch him just looking in my direction while we work. Always looking out for me. Today, he's weirdly distant and avoidant. That's my fault, clearly. Stupid big mouth.

What on earth got into me? I don't think of him that way, do I? I mean, I like him. I might even love him. But we've only ever been friends. He's certainly never showed any romantic interest in me, so where did I even get the idea to suggest something dumb like that?

Maybe I was just feeling lonely and desperate. Finding out about the dating show project, plus hearing about Ethan and Sarah… These two things might have stirred up some feelings that needed soothing. Adding way too much alcohol to the mix certainly didn't help.

Damien just happened to be the closest and—I thought—safest person to turn to. So much for that.

Seeing as he's still acting weird today, he wasn't as safe as my drunken self from last night wanted to believe.

Maybe the best thing for our friendship will be to ignore it ever happened and never speak of it again. Friends with benefits. Me and Damien? Forget it!

Though… I can see it. *Kind of.* But also really not. He's handsome, in a cuddly and soft kind of way. Sweet. Caring. Generous. And I love how much taller he is compared to me. How he towers over me. How safe he makes me feel when we're together. I can usually tell what he's thinking or what he's going to say before he does.

But that's not *sexy*, is it? That's just… Familiar and comfortable.

Damien is a lot of things, but he's not mysterious anymore. Maybe I need that. And maybe he needs it too, and that's why he balked at my drunken suggestion.

But we did end up cuddling. A lot. And it was lovely. Maybe drunk Jill had it all figured out. Best friends and cuddle buddies? That should be attainable.

Only if I mend this rift between us somehow. Today is our last day as coworkers until the new project starts. We should hang out like we usually do between shoots. Meet up and catch some Netflix at home, or go to the cinema. Maybe have a nice meal somewhere…

Not as a date, just as best friends.

I'm going to give him some space before bringing it up. Let the awkwardness fade. We've been so close these past few years, I'm not going to let one drunken conversation ruin everything we have.

CHAPTER FOUR

*** Damien ***

Getting up early for work has always been a mixed bag of feelings for me.

On the one hand, I'm not a morning person, so it's painful.

On the other, usually around this time of day, I'm heading to a set somewhere and looking forward to those precious moments between takes which I get to spend with Jill.

The work is fine; I enjoy most of it. But the highlight is always that little tea break. The shared lunch. A little chat here or there, recapping everything we've just witnessed on set. Making a joke or snarky remark in passing, and rejoicing when I manage to make her laugh. Or just sitting side by side in silence to recover at the end of a hectic day.

It's so comfortable. So effortless. Our friendship gives me something to look forward to every single day, but it also reminds me of everything that will never be.

This morning is different, though. It's our first day off after *Decadent Desserts* unexpectedly got cut short.

The first morning in a couple of months where I get to sleep in and relax, and yet I'm not doing either of those things. I kept tossing and turning for what felt like hours last night. And even though it's criminal to be up this early on a Sunday morning, I still can't sleep another wink.

I keep *thinking*. Ruminating.

I keep replaying the events of the past couple of days. Or rather, my memories of the Uber ride after the farewell party the day before, and Jill's weird behavior yesterday while wrapping up on set. And once I'm done obsessing about those two moments in time, I cycle back to how she acted after Claire made the announcement about the new show.

Maybe she did regret foregoing her promotion to get me onto the new crew.

Maybe her remarks in the car about 'benefits' was a test of some sort, and I unknowingly did or said something to offend her.

But then, she was curled up in my arms the entire way home that night. The. Entire. Way. And whenever I allow myself to dwell on that for a while, my body reacts in a most inappropriate way.

And then she didn't speak a word of it the following day. What does *that* mean? Was that the real test? Was *I* supposed to say something and I didn't, so now she feels bad? Or was she regretting that it ever happened?

BEST FRIENDS FOREVER

If only I knew how to interpret any of this. Women are a mystery to me. What do they even want? Not me, obviously. They don't tend to want me. But what *do* they want? If I knew that, I wouldn't be single anymore.

And why can't any of them just *say* what they really mean instead of leaving me guessing?

I want to message her like I normally would on my day off. Ask what she's up to. If she wants to meet up, maybe. Talk about Sarah's article, which got published yesterday afternoon while we were still on set. It was an eye-opener, and how she described her first impressions of Ethan on the *Decadent Desserts* set was the single most romantic thing I've ever read in my whole life. I didn't even realize the two of them had become a couple.

But I can't silence the little voice in my head telling me that Jill is glad to be rid of me today. That she'd only engage me because she's being polite. She's probably relieved to get a chance to forget about the awkwardness that has developed between us.

Maybe I should tell her I'd be okay with it if she tells Claire she's changed her mind about that assistant. I'll find another job at some point. No big deal.

I'm a single guy living in a small house share in a cheap part of town. The savings I have will tide me over until I get another contract. It'll be fine. As long as she doesn't resent me anymore and we can at least stay friends. *Without* any so-called benefits.

But I don't do any of that. Instead, I pick up my phone and start doom scrolling on Facebook. And I lose hours of my morning that way, without feeling any better.

Just when I want to put it down and maybe try to get to sleep again after all, an ad catches my attention.

Millions of couples have already found love…

The picture of the smiling twenty-something man and woman underneath gives me pause. If I squint and hold the phone an arm's length away, he kind of looks like me.

Ad targeting has become scary these last few years. It's as if the phone has peered inside the deepest corners of my subconscious and figured out just what I really need.

I want to be part of one of those 'millions of couples'. Like Ethan and Sarah, who seemingly fell in love overnight under our very noses last week, if her article is to be believed!

I want to be the guy in the picture, with his arms around a woman who looks at him like he's her everything. Kind of like how I held Jill in the back of the car. *No, shut up! Not at all like Jill and I in the car; we're just friends!*

I want this so much it hurts. And the ad is for an app I'd tried a couple of years ago, anyway. I'd just have to make sure the profile is up-to-date and re-up my subscription. It's almost too easy. Certainly too easy to pass up in this moment of weakness.

Just like that, my plan to waste time on social media until I fall asleep again has been abandoned, and I dive headfirst into the world of online dating. Again.

Hope is a weird and wonderful thing.

Before long, I've tweaked my written profile and shortlisted a few newer photos of myself to replace the outdated one from before. Now, the big question is: which one out of these do I pick as the main profile picture? I have zero self-awareness about this, so I instinctively navigate to my WhatsApp conversation with Jill, send her the two contending images, and ask which is better for a dating profile. Send. And wait.

This is safe, right? It signals that I'm not going to dwell on that conversation in the cab home. That further awkwardness is unnecessary.

No read-receipt. No response. She's not a morning person either, so this doesn't mean anything, does it? No matter how weird things are between us, she'd never refuse to help with stuff like this… She's probably still asleep, I convince myself. At least I've taken the first step and reached out to her while also trying to better my own life. Two birds, one stone.

I put my phone down, lie back against my pillow,

and stare at the ceiling. I've made a start. Who knows, hopefully this attempt at online dating will end better than the last.

There are plenty of fish in the sea, right? I just have to find the one that's right for *me*. One that isn't Jill.

* Jill *

I had planned to talk it out with Damien today, on the first day off after our cancelled contract. Reach out. Clear the air, and hopefully get back to how things used to be between us. But before I get that chance, I wake up to an unexpected phone call from Claire instead.

"Morning, sunshine. I didn't wake you, did I?" she teases.

I blink a few times and glance at the clock. It's barely eight. She interrupted a most wonderful dream. About Damien. Damien and me. Doing things we would never ever do in real life…

"Nope, I'm fine. Just about to head to the gym," I lie. *Me*. Going to the gym at eight. *As if.*

"Right. Well, I wouldn't have bothered you this early on your day off, but as you know, TV never sleeps. My meeting at the network has been pushed up to noon today, and I was wondering if you'd want to tag along."

Suddenly my eyes are wide open. Work on the new show must be moving faster than I thought. "A meeting? Sure. What do you need me to do?"

"Wear something professional, bring a large reporter pad, and be ready to take a bunch of notes."

"I can do that."

"I know you can. That's why I'm telling you." Claire sounds stern, but as I've gotten to know her these past few months, I recognize that it's just an act. I can hear a hint of a smile in her voice.

"Cool."

"What's the last dating show you watched?" she asks.

I close my eyes for a moment and think. "That game show type thing. With what's-his-face."

"*Take Me Out*?" Claire asks.

That's the one! "Yes."

"It's been off air for a year, but okay. And?"

"The blind date show with the pods on Netflix."

"Great. Before you arrive for the meeting, make a list of every major dating show that's aired over the last, say, five years, and write a couple of sentences outlining each concept. I want to make sure that our new project doesn't obviously rip anyone off."

"Perfect. I'll have it all ready. Where do we meet?" I ask.

Claire rattles off the directions while I type them into a note on my phone. By the time she hangs up,

I'm fully alert and calculating backwards. I've less than four hours to get there. Factoring in public transport, taking a shower, ironing my one and only professional outfit…

It's tight, but it's fine. When you work in this industry, you become used to deadlines. Ignoring all the random notifications, emails, and any other icons on my phone, I quickly set an alarm and start compiling the list Claire asked for. With the help of various showbiz news websites, including the one that reporter, Sarah, works for, I have a comprehensive list ready within a couple of hours.

Hopefully it's enough to satisfy Claire, because my alarm goes off, meaning I have to start getting ready. Another half hour later, I'm showered, sort of dressed, and ready to leave. I grab a couple of granola bars to eat on the way, and I'm off.

A production meeting at the network. My first one! I'm moving up in the world!

By the time I make it to the station and onto the right train, my adrenaline is still pumping. I watch the sunlit scenery zip past the window and take a moment to breathe, before taking out my phone and sending an update to Claire.

'On the train now. I've made the list you asked for. See you there!'

Send.

Only then do I start checking the various

notifications that have piled up overnight, including some messages from Damien from a couple of hours ago. That's awfully early for him, especially on his day off...

I feel a strange sensation while I let my finger hover over his name. A buzzing feeling in my chest. A lingering memory of the dream Claire interrupted in which we were—

I open the chat and find two selfies inside. One from the *Decadent Desserts* set, and one from Comic Con or something like that. Seeing them makes me smile.

Below, he asks which will be better for a dating profile. And the corners of my mouth drop again.

I check the timestamp on the messages again. Is he really working on his profile this early in the morning? That's a bit... desperate.

I frown at the phone, then look up and stare out the window for a bit. Maybe that awkward Uber ride home stirred some things up for him as well. Seeing as he clearly wasn't into *me*—hell, I'm not even sure I'm into him that way—I guess it's only fair he should try his luck elsewhere. Still, my heart feels inexplicably heavy.

Not that I don't want him to find happiness; I do! But internet dating is such a shit show normally. The unanswered messages. The blind dates gone wrong. I remember him telling me about one girl he met via one of those apps who seemed perfect in every way. They chatted for a couple of months, until she stood him up on their first date and completely ghosted him after…

I don't know. The entire situation just stinks. And I don't want him to get hurt.

But we're friends. And friends are supposed to be supportive. The last thing I want is to annoy him just when he's trying to reach out to me.

I take a deep breath and reply to the Comic Con picture.

'This one will be perfect! What else are you up to today? I'm heading into town to meet with Claire at the network. Maybe we can grab dinner once I'm back?'

I stare at the phone for a little while, but I'm not even sure the message has been sent at all. Stupid patchy network.

Ugh. I shrug and put the phone back in my shoulder bag, before scanning the largely empty train carriage. There aren't too many people out and about this early on a Sunday. Why would they be? Normal folk don't work weekends. They might be enjoying a quiet day in with the family, or planning a summer barbecue. Or in case they're really enterprising, perhaps an outing to the seaside…

Normally I might have felt like I'm missing out. But every time I think about where I'm going—an important meeting at the network—I feel that same spark of excitement all over again. This is what I wanted: a chance to move up in my career.

Nothing—not even missing a chance to enjoy the glorious weather or the idea of Damien jumping back into the online dating pool—is going to ruin my mood today!

CHAPTER FIVE

* Jill *

I make it to the agreed meeting point exactly on time. It's a little coffee shop which I'm sure does great business on weekdays among the takeout crowd. But this morning, there's hardly anyone inside. I decide to wait out by the door, catching a few rays of sun as I do.

By the time I take a few deep breaths, smooth down the wrinkles that have developed on my outfit during the train journey, and organize my notes in my bag, Claire makes an appearance as well.

"You're here. Wonderful," she says while checking her watch.

It's always straight to business with her. I suppress a smile. It makes me wonder what she'd be like in her down time, or worse still, on a date! I really cannot imagine Claire on a date.

"Do you want to go through the list right now?" I ask.

She takes a seat at one of the small table-and-chair arrangements dotting the pavement outside the coffee shop. I place my notepad in front of her.

"The usual, black coffee, two sugars?" I ask, before stepping inside.

She nods absentmindedly while scanning the page I'd prepared and mumbling a few things under her breath.

I order our drinks in to-go cups and am back outside before she even realizes it. A black coffee for her and a normal tea with milk for me. No frills. No time wastage.

"Hope I didn't miss anything important. It was the best I could do given the timeframe," I remark, putting her cup down in front of her and taking a seat on the other chair.

"No, no, this is great." Claire looks up at me. "I meant to explain, this meeting was supposed to be next week. But you know how it is. A few things got moved around, and here we are today, with hardly any notice."

I nod. "It's not a problem."

Somewhere in my bag, my phone rings once.

"Do you need to take that?" she asks.

"It's probably just Damien replying to a message I'd sent him. I'll switch my sound off before we go into the meeting."

She nods briefly, but keeps eyeing me suspiciously until I just can't ignore it anymore.

"What?" I ask, putting the muted phone away again.

As she raises the paper cup to her pursed lips, I think I see a strange glint in her eye. "Ah, good coffee."

I continue frowning at her.

"Have your tea, it's almost time to go!" she urges.

"Uh-huh." I reluctantly take a sip. It's still a tad hot for my liking.

"It's just, you and Damien. I was wondering when that would happen," she remarks, just when I swallow.

I put the cup down a little too fast in protest. Thankfully the lid doesn't allow its contents to slosh out. "We're just friends!"

"Right."

"Really! Damien? No! I mean, he's a nice guy, but… No!"

"First you get me to hire him for this new show, and then you guys leave the pub together after the *Decadent Desserts* farewell drinks… It's totally fine; there aren't any rules about stuff like this like in other jobs. It's your life." She shrugs. "I think you guys make a cute couple."

I sit back and glance at her, and then back at my drink, still shaking my head. "It's nothing like that. We're just really good friends."

"I see. Is that what he told you?"

I frown again. As if I'd let a guy dictate terms in the way she's suggesting!

"That's what *I* say. I'm assuming he feels the same way." His reaction to my inappropriate suggestion in the cab and the announcement that he's going to be dating again are obvious proof that my assumption is correct.

So what if I woke up this morning to a suggestive dream with him in the starring role? That's totally normal, right? Everyone has naughty dreams about male friends or coworkers sometimes, don't they? That's just biology. It's hormones; it doesn't *mean* anything!

In any case, it takes two to tango. And he's not into it.

"Okay, Jill. Anyway, it's time. Let's see what we're up against," Claire says, while pushing her chair back.

I hurriedly collect my research and stuff it in my bag before picking up my tea. It takes me a minute to regain my composure and ask something I should have led with, rather than allow her to ambush me about my non-relationship with Damien.

"Roughly how much talking do you want me to do in there?" I ask while we start walking towards Home TV's shiny glass-fronted building further up the road.

She smiles at me, takes a large final sip of coffee, and discards the cup in a nearby trash can.

"You've done the research, right? Talk whenever you have something to add. It'll be fine."

"Thanks, Claire," I say.

"Let's go!" She smiles at me, then we pick up the pace, our heels click-clacking furiously against the pavement as we walk the rest of the way to our destination.

I still can't believe it. My first network meeting! The fact that Claire trusts me for this is encouraging. I guess over the past couple of months I've done *something* right on set.

* Damien *

Since I didn't hear from Jill in time, I ended up uploading both of the chosen photos to my newly reactivated dating profile, and then I went back to bed. Maybe it was exhaustion, or just the sense that I'm taking responsibility for my own happiness, but I managed to get a good couple of hours of sleep after that.

When I wake up, I finally feel rested. Like this might be the beginning of a new chapter after all. We have a couple of weeks off before work on the new show starts. Who knows, by then I might have gone on a few dates already. Maybe then I'll finally appreciate Jill's company for what it really is: a wonderful friendship that's perfect just the way it is. Without adding complications and expectations to it which neither of us really needs.

It's a beautiful summer's day, and the sun is

already streaming in through the kinks in the curtains. A few sounds coming from the other side of the door alert me to the fact that my roommates must also be up by now. Due to our different work schedules, we don't see too much of each other normally, and that's okay with me.

I'm secretly envious of Jill, who managed to move into a small flat of her own last year. I guess her pay is a little higher than mine. Or she hasn't got the same level of student loans I have to contend with.

Whatever it is. It's something I've been working towards for a while now.

The sounds beyond the door fade a little, and I finally emerge from my room as well and head to the shared kitchen. It's reassuringly quiet, so I make myself comfortable, eager to properly start the day.

When my phone buzzes halfway through breakfast, I fully expect it to be Jill. I mean, who else would it be? It isn't, though. There's a new yet vaguely familiar icon in my notification bar. The dating app.

Filled with equal measures of excitement and trepidation, I click on the icon and wait for it to load. A new chat has come in from someone named *heather91*.

I stare at the phone in shock for a moment. That name! I know her! She was the whole reason I quit dating in the first place… Well, her, and my developing feelings for Jill. Two reasons, technically.

Although the memory of what happened between us frustrates me all over again, I can't contain my curiosity and open the chat anyway. I hold my breath while I start to read.

'Damien, OMG! How are you? Where have you been? I've thought about you so much these last couple of years. I thought you blocked me, or something had happened to you… Anyway, let's reconnect and catch up, what do you say? Heather. '

I don't quite know how to react to that. She thought I blocked *her*? As I remember, she's the one who stood *me* upon our first in-person date and ghosted *me*for at least a week after, so I'm not sure how she got the opposite idea.

Still baffled, and a little pissed off, I start typing a response.

'Heather. Well, after waiting for you for two hours at the restaurant, and not hearing anything despite my numerous messages, I assumed we had run our course. I cancelled my subscription and decided to focus on my career.'

Too much? Holding grudges isn't healthy or attractive, but then again, I think I'm justified in this case. I send it anyway.

And soon after, the little icon next to her name

turns green to signal she's also logged on.

I wonder what she'll say to that. I don't have to wait long for her reply.

'Yeah, about that, I'm soooo sorry! The dumbest thing happened that day. I got into an accident on the way to our date. It wasn't too bad, but I did have to stay in the hospital for about a week. My phone got damaged too, so I couldn't reach out until I got a new one… And by then… Well, I guess it was too late, because you had completely vanished. Until I saw your profile pop back up this morning!'

My heart starts to race as I read her explanation. I lean back in my chair and push my plate away. Jesus. Now *I* feel like the villain, and suddenly I'm not hungry anymore.

'I'm so sorry that happened to you! I guess I fucked up, huh?' I type.

I close my eyes and try to remember what she was like. After messaging back and forth for a couple of months, we had only just agreed to meet for the first time. It wasn't a full-fledged relationship yet by the time circumstance broke us apart. But it was the closest I had come to one in years. We had potential, didn't we? It felt that way to me, anyway. We would message for hours every single day.

It hurt when she seemingly stood me up, so I'd told myself a bunch of stories to feel better. That we were incompatible. That I was starting to develop feelings for Jill and shouldn't be dating someone else, anyway…

But how will I ever get over my fascination with Jill if I don't give someone else a chance? Or am I going to waste what's left of my twenties pining for someone who doesn't like me back? How pathetic would that be?

Very pathetic, I decide.

'What do you say we start over?' I suggest.

Her reply is as prompt as ever.

':) Yes, let's do that. But first you tell me what you've been up to since we last spoke,' she writes.

So I do. I tell her about my work—at least those parts not currently covered by any NDAs—and ask about her life as well. Before I know it, an hour passes and we're still talking. It's nice. Like those two years in between didn't even happen. And by the time I finally do get up to put my dirty dishes away, we've even set a day and time for our *next* first date: the coming Friday.

CHAPTER SIX

The meeting at the network passes by in a blur. So much to discuss; so many notes to take.

By the time I've said my goodbyes to Claire and I'm on the train home again, I finally take a moment to reflect.

The schedule for the new show has been moved up. We have less time and an even smaller budget. But Claire isn't someone who gets flustered by such things. And her confidence seems to be rubbing off on me. If she thinks we can do it, that means we can.

When I finally check my phone again, I have a message from Damien waiting for me as well. Dinner is on; my place as usual, thanks to my lack of roommates. Whew. I guess he's no longer weirded out.

I have just enough time to grab some groceries on the way home, type up my notes from the meeting for Claire, and change into something more casual, and then the doorbell rings, alerting me to Damien's arrival.

"Hey!" I greet him at the door with a wide smile

on my face.

He reciprocates, and holds up a six-pack of craft ales. "Thought we should celebrate!"

That's so sweet; Damien in a nutshell.

"Perfect! I was in the mood to order pizza tonight. Who wants to cook in this weather, huh?"

Damien chuckles. "Or any weather, right?"

He knows me too well. I'm not exactly a domestic goddess.

"Sit! I'll get us something to munch on while we decide what to order," I tell him, pointing at the shabby couch gracing my modest open plan living area. He puts the beer down on the coffee table, and sits back while sighing contentedly.

"As ugly as this thing is, it sure is comfy," he remarks.

"It came with the flat," I remind him.

"Yeah, along with everything else."

This is a running joke between us. When I moved in here last year I had hardly anything in terms of furniture or other belongings. It's been a work-in-progress, and I've just been too busy to really put my own mark on the place. Still, at least I don't have roommates anymore. A luxury poor Damien is still saving up for so far.

I join him on the couch, carrying a selection of potato chips and other snacks, and he hands me an open bottle of beer.

"So, what happened at the meeting?" he asks. "What's going on with this new show?"

"Oh, where do I even begin?" I exclaim.

"At the beginning. Cheers," he says, while we clink our bottles together.

I take a sip, smile, and do exactly that. I tell him about Claire waking me up in the morning and about the research I had to do, then arriving at the network only to find that nobody had told reception about our meeting. And when we finally reached the right conference room, we found that there was an unexpected third person already waiting with the network execs: the guy who had come up with the concept for the show before Claire ever got involved.

I tell Damien that the show is going to be called *Sealed with a Kiss* and it's going to be blind first dates in a restaurant setting, but with a catch. All the contestants will have been matched to each other with some kind of psychometric test devised by that therapist guy we have to work with. That's what will make it unique.

Damien raises an eyebrow. "So it's going to be all scientific? What makes couples compatible?"

"Apparently. He wants to have a little segment on air for himself, explaining what worked and what didn't. Breaking down a different aspect of attraction or compatibility in each episode. Claire said that'll be too preachy. It won't have mass appeal and will ruin the magic of love at first sight, which most viewers find so attractive about these sorts of shows, but the suits at the network seemed to disagree with her."

"Huh," Damien responds. "And what do *you* think?"

I take another sip of beer while mulling it over.

"I think firstly we don't have a choice, and secondly, I'm sure we could edit it in such a way that it captures people's interest. Plus, I'm kind of curious about what he has to say, you know?"

"Yeah… It could be helpful. For those of us who lack the inbuilt talent to get through a date without making absolute fools of ourselves!"

"Oh, you can't think that way!" I protest. "Now you tell me about what *you've* been up to today? Online dating, huh?"

He smiles mysteriously before grabbing some potato chips from the bag I'm holding up in his direction.

"Can you believe it, I've already got a date lined up, actually!"

I stare at him for a second. "Whoa. That was quick!"

"Don't sound so shocked that someone wants to date me!" He shoots me a disapproving look.

I shake my head. "No, I don't mean it like that!" Ugh, me and my big mouth. The last thing I wanted was to make him feel bad.

"I'm happy for you, I just need more details, that's all," I say.

Of course Damien has a date already. He's a great guy! It just… stings. And I don't quite understand why. Was Claire right? Is our relationship maybe not as clear cut as I want to believe?

Damien clears his throat. "So, actually, I haven't told you the whole story yet. It's actually Heather. I think I told you about her."

I frown and try to think. *Heather, Heather, Heather… Oh, damn!*

"No way! Not the girl who ghosted you years ago?" I ask.

"That's the one. But she had a very good reason," he says.

Excuse, surely. I give him the suspicious side-eye while grabbing some chips for myself.

"She had gotten into an accident on the way to our date, and because her phone got damaged, she couldn't let me know about what happened. I guess I overreacted when I shut down my profile." Damien's expression tenses up while he speaks.

"You couldn't possibly guess all that!" I tell him, while placing my hand on his arm. Oh, that feels… funny. "For all you know, she vanished on you!"

"Yeah, but maybe I should have given her the benefit of the doubt. We'd been talking for a couple of months by then."

He really does seem to feel guilty, and I don't like it. He's being way too hard on himself. Plus, the whole 'I got into an accident on the way' excuse sounds rather too convenient. Like she regretted dumping him back then and fed him a bunch of bullshit to cover up for it. Surely she could have logged into her old account on her new phone? Only a nice guy like Damien would fall for that.

"This is why long-distance stuff never works," I say. "It's impossible to really know someone's intentions if you can't see their body language or anything. Unless you're video chatting."

"Right."

"Have you been? Video chatting, I mean?"

He shakes his head. "No, just chat."

I have some thoughts about that, but I keep my mouth shut. "When is this long-overdue first date finally happening?" I ask instead.

He shrugs awkwardly. "Friday night."

I smile briefly. "Well, I wish you all the best for it."

Screw that. She doesn't deserve him, not after what she did! She might have told him a story about some kind of accident, but I'm not buying it. And the fact that they've never even done a video chat makes me even more suspicious. Maybe she's catfishing him. And if that's the case, I'm definitely not going to forgive her, and I hope he doesn't either.

If she messes up again, I'll have her head on a

pike.

*** Damien ***

It's such a relief, chilling on the ugly sofa at Jill's place, like nothing ever happened. All the weirdness of the recent past has been forgotten. I knew it. I should have taken action earlier.

Maybe my own desperation had reached such pathetic heights that it started affecting our entire relationship. Maybe that's what the whole Uber incident was about?

Either way, we're back to normal now. Things are once again comfortable, at least at her end. Because every so often, I'm still dealing with all the unwanted feelings I can't seem to fully ignore.

Try what you may, you don't simply fall out of love with someone just because you've decided to. It's a process, one that might take a while.

Still, we're having a nice time together. Pizza, beer, and Netflix. And a whole lot of random conversation in between episodes of *Stranger Things*.

By the time the sun has finally set, we're spread out across the full length of the big sofa. She's curled up and almost lying down against one armrest, and I'm pushed into the opposing corner with my feet up on the coffee table, when I survey the leftovers of our dinner.

Empty pizza box. Empty bottles. Empty nacho

bag. We can be such teenagers sometimes.

"What about dessert?" I ask.

"You're still hungry?" Jill stretches her legs, almost brushing her feet against my thigh. Jesus, that's a bit close for comfort. My body reacts instantly, and panic washes over me.

I quickly shake my head. "Not hungry per se. Just… craving something sweet." And desperate to get up off the sofa, before I end up doing something I regret. Like rubbing her feet, or…

"I think there's some ice cream in the freezer," she says.

I raise an eyebrow, grateful for the opening. "You *think?* Who on earth doesn't *know* whether they've got ice cream?"

She chuckles. I love the sound of her laughter. I wonder what her voice would sound like during… *Oh lord, give me strength!*

"Give me a break. Today is the first day in weeks that I've been home in time for dinner!" she argues.

"Uh huh. So, I guess you don't want any, then?" I tease, getting up from my seat. It's a little awkward with a semi, but necessary. Before things escalate out of control.

"I didn't say that!" she complains.

"Right." I bite my lip, hard, while walking past her and stealing a glance at her pretty face. She's tired, just like that night… God, I wish I could hold her like that again.

Seeing her this way does something to me. Like it's my responsibility to take care of her, which is ridiculous. On set, she's usually the capable one. Apparently, I can't even get myself hired without her help.

It takes me a good few minutes to shake off all these lingering thoughts while rummaging around in her freezer for that forgotten tub of ice cream, all the way at the back. I divide its contents somewhat equally into two mismatched bowls from the drying rack and I'm back.

Jill is falling asleep from the looks of it. She's adorable. Like a blonde angel resting after a long day of being absolutely perfect. For a split second I'm tempted to lean over her and plant a kiss on her forehead. Thankfully I have the presence of mind to stop myself.

I take care not to wake her as I sit down, but still she stirs, and gets up onto her elbows.

"You found it," she remarks, shooting a sleepy smile my way.

"Here." I hand her a bowl and a spoon, which she accepts with both hands.

Our fingers brush past each other and I forget to breathe. Her eyes pause on mine for a moment. Did she notice? How my heart skips a few beats every time she comes near me? Can she tell how very close

I am to leaning over in her direction and kissing her?

She smiles again and sits up with the bowl in her hands. "Thanks, you're the best."

Am I? Then why are we just friends? Why can't we be more than that, dammit?

She must have picked up on the sudden change in my mood, because she immediately questions it.

"What's wrong?"

I shake my head. "Nothing. I should probably head home after this. It's late." Plus, it's the only way to avoid me saying or doing something I'll regret.

She nods, slowly eating her first spoonful of ice cream. "Mmm… Tastes of freezer."

I briefly force a smile and nod. "It does. Good thing we're finishing it now."

Speaking of finishing stuff. I think I know what to do now. It was nice spending the evening here at Jill's place, but it also really wasn't. Because every moment of it hurts, in some measure or other.

Despite thinking I'd figured a genius way out of this pit of despair I'm in, simply deciding to date Heather wasn't enough to fix *this*. To give Heather and me a good chance, I'm going to need to keep my distance from Jill, just long enough to get over her once and for all.

CHAPTER SEVEN

* Jill *

Since that Sunday, I've hardly heard from Damien. There have been the occasional messages back and forth, but whenever I try to make a plan to meet up, he's always busy. Meeting family, which normally he *never* does, or he's already made a plan to talk to Heather all evening. I try not to read too much into it, but I've never known him to be busy like this.

Maybe he's trying to make the most of our time off, because mid-shoot he would never get the chance for all of this stuff? Or has that earlier awkwardness made a reappearance?

A whole week passes where we don't see each other at all. After spending the past couple of months together on set every single day, this is not just weird; it hurts.

I miss him. Every day and every night. And the more I do, the more I dream of him. Of us.

And all the while, there's a voice in the back of my head convincing me that things will only get worse from here. Once he gets serious with that Heather woman, I might just lose him forever. Who knows, she might be one of those possessive girlfriends who won't understand that her boyfriend has a female best friend. The bitch! I know nothing much about her, and yet I hate her already.

It's not healthy. And perhaps that's why Damien doesn't want to spend time with me anymore. He can probably tell that I disapprove of his budding relationship… And now I feel guilty about it. Guilty for projecting my own ugly feelings onto her and especially *him*.

God, I wish I knew a way out of this mess. A way back to my best friend, whom I haven't seen in a week, except during those blissful moments in between sleeping and waking, when I can still pretend that we're fine. And we're so much more than just friends.

The worst part is, he hasn't *said* anything as such. He might genuinely be busy, while I'm over here driving myself crazy and making a mountain out of nothing.

On top of that, I have nothing much to do all day. That first meeting at the network was just that. A first meeting. Unlike what it sounded like, it didn't kick start anything just yet. And I've had such a busy schedule for so long that I don't remember how to do leisure time anymore.

I'm starting to wonder if the project has fallen through altogether, when Claire calls me on this otherwise dull and dreary Monday morning.

"Hey! Busy?" she asks.

The lack of 'how are you?' or any other niceties almost gets on my nerves, but I shake it off with a deep breath. Claire is calling. This is *good,* right?

"Not busy. What's up?" I say.

Claire pauses for a moment on the other end, then clears her throat. "Can you come meet me at my office?"

I frown. "You have an office? When did this happen?"

"Sorry, yeah, I figured now that I'm in charge of my own show, I should set up in a dedicated place, rather than meet people at local cafes. It's near Hammersmith tube station, in one of those shared office buildings for freelancers."

"Congratulations!" I say.

She doesn't immediately respond. I hear the rustling of paper.

"I'm on the phone with her right now, hang on," she speaks in a muffled voice.

"Claire?"

"When can you get here?" she asks.

I shrug and check the time. Hammersmith. That's not far. "Do you need me to research or prepare or do anything?"

"Nope, just grace me with your esteemed presence and we'll take it from there."

Despite the heavy dose of snark and sarcasm in her answer, I'm still smiling. It's good to be needed. Plus, I'm desperate for the distraction. "Forty minutes, max."

"Okay. See you." The line goes silent almost immediately, leaving me wondering what just happened.

Oh yeah. I've got to go! A part of me is grateful to get out of the house. If Claire is calling, that means there's movement. And if there's movement, then I'll soon be too damn busy to think about what went wrong with Damien.

Plus, the moment we start shooting, we'll be back on set together anyway. It'll be like nothing ever happened, and we'll be back to normal in no time. Maybe then those stupid dreams will also stop.

*** Damien ***

For a week I've been suffering on my own, though it feels much longer than that. Since I don't have many friends outside of work anymore, my self-imposed distance from Jill has been rough.

Sure, my renewed contact with Heather has kept me occupied some of the time. And it's been nice. But what I've needed at least as much is a confidante to share with. To discuss this new-old relationship; to see if there's any hope of it leading somewhere. And to come up with a solid first date strategy. It was supposed to happen on Friday, but something came up, so it's been postponed by one week, buying me more time. Not that extra time is going to do me any good if I don't have a sounding board to bounce ideas off of!

What do I even talk about? What will I wear? *Ugh!*

I keep reminding myself that it's all for a good cause. I'll be a better friend to Jill if I can get my head right and figure out life on my own. And I'll definitely be a better boyfriend to Heather, when we finally do meet. But… it's becoming increasingly difficult to follow through, because I'm beginning to feel like a failure at both.

It's Monday morning, and I'm up too early and staring at the ceiling. My roommates have just left for work and the rest of the house is eerily quiet. What will I even do with myself all day? Video games or Netflix? I'm so damn bored of it all.

Half of the morning drags on like this. I find myself sitting alone in the shared kitchen, staring at my baked beans on toast rather than eating them, when my phone starts to ring.

It sounds so loud in the otherwise empty house that the sound startles me. My heart actually skips a couple of beats when I see that it's Gavin. Finally! If he's calling, that means there's some work to do. Or I'm fired. Hopefully it's the former.

"Damien. Sorry to disturb your exciting holiday schedule. What have you got going on today?" Gavin greets me. Sort of.

"What's up, boss? Nothing much, just having some fo—"

"Just kidding, mate; I don't care what you're doing. We've got work to do!" His tone leaves little room for argument.

Who am I kidding; I'm thrilled to get out of the house! I take a large sip of Coke to wash down the partially-chewed remnants of toast.

"Okay. What do you need?" I ask, pushing my mostly full plate away from me. Whatever it is, I'm ready.

"Tell you what. I'm going to text you an address. Be there in half an hour," Gavin says.

"Okay…" Mysterious!

"It's Claire's office," Gavin clarifies. "Crew meeting."

"Right." Well maybe not *so* mysterious after all. But that's good, right? Finally, we've got a show to shoot. It feels like my life has purpose again.

"Jill is also on the way," Gavin adds.

Ah. Well. That shouldn't surprise me, but it catches me off-guard anyway. "Okay, I'll be there shortly."

"Thirty minutes!" Gavin reminds me.

"Okay, boss," I say. But the line has gone dead

already. He's never been the patient type.

Just like that, the lazy morning that just wouldn't pass has been turned upside-down. I quickly eat my second toast, clear the table, and rush into the bedroom to get ready. Shave or shower? I glance in the mirror, dismayed at the disheveled reflection looking back at me. I literally haven't shaved once this past week, and it's showing.

Meanwhile, the phone alerts me to Gavin's incoming text. I put the address into Google Maps and try to figure out just how I'm going to get there on time. If only I didn't have to rely on public transport… Ugh.

In the end, I barely have time to get dressed and brush my teeth; they'll just have to deal with the seven-day-stubble I'm sporting.

***

I reach the building housing Claire's office seven minutes late. When I finally make it to the correct floor and cabin, I can hear a handful of people already arguing back and forth loudly.

"Okay, well, we have to get the auditions on tape. You never know what gems we might discover in there," Claire says.

"Claire is right," Jill says. "Look at *X Factor*. The auditions are the best part."

"We're not shooting the next *X Factor*," Gavin grumbles.

The temptation to ask what's going on passes as soon as I enter right in the middle of the fray. Claire is leaning against her desk; Gavin is sitting on one of the few chairs. There's a guy wearing a tweed jacket whom I've never seen before sitting behind the desk. Jill is perched on the armrest of the small sofa in the corner of the office with a large notepad balancing on her knee.

And every single one of them turns around and looks at me when I enter through the rather flimsy aluminum-framed door. Jill gives me a little wave.

"Guess I made it to the right place," I mumble to myself, while nodding at Jill, who smiles at me.

"Damien. You're late." Gavin folds his arms in front of his chest. He doesn't look too pissed off, though.

"The tube takes as long as it takes, boss." I shrug.

"You're lucky you're already hired," he grumbles.

Right. Guess I have Jill to thank for that.

"So, have we got a start date?" I ask, taking a seat on the only empty spot in the whole room: on the sofa, next to Jill.

Claire starts chewing on her bottom lip like she does when she's lost in thought. "I still think we should get the auditions on tape. What do you think, Owen?" she turns to the new guy, who briefly makes eye contact with me and nods.

I reciprocate.

Jill leans over in my direction. "That's the therapist I was telling you about. It's basically all his idea, this show," she whispers.

"I think you're right. The more we get the patients—sorry, contestants—to talk on camera, the better it will be. And I'd need to see all the raw footage, so I can really dive deep in my own on-camera analyses."

Claire turns to Gavin. "Well, there you go. Decision made."

"We've already got applications coming in from all over the country. We'll do a day of auditions locally, and one in Glasgow," Claire adds. "Since we're on a tight schedule, I would like to conduct them simultaneously."

"God," Gavin scoffs.

"Lucky for me, I have two teams ready," Claire says with a triumphant grin on her face.

She does? I frown and look over at Jill, who is nodding slowly while scribbling down some notes. A few locks of her hair escape before she pushes them back again. As she does that, a whiff of her floral perfume hits me. It's making me lose focus and think of things I definitely shouldn't be thinking about. Like our drive home after the crew get-together just over a week ago… And the many inappropriate dreams I've had since, which featured her in the starring role.

What would have happened if I'd reacted differently on that night? We were both drunk, but what if I'd said yes anyway?

"I'm not going to Glasgow," Gavin complains.

"Fine. Damien and Jill will go," Claire says. "You will shoot the auditions here with me."

I nod in agreement. Sounds good. Jill, however, stops writing mid-sentence.

"You want me to handle the auditions in Glasgow? By myself?" she asks.

"Who else? You're the only other producer on the show," Claire says.

Jill leans back and hugs the notepad to her body. "Okay!"

The genuine excitement in her voice makes me smile. This is a big responsibility, and everyone in the room knows it. I'm so damn proud of her it's making my chest hurt.

"Okay, so Jill, if you don't mind booking the train tickets and a hotel, and put word out to all the applicants and tell them to be ready this Saturday, I'll contact the network to get studio space blocked off for the day in Glasgow as well as here and figure out the exact schedule."

Claire's instructions prompt Jill back into action. She quickly notes down a few bullet points in her journal and looks up with a wide grin on her face.

"Done!" Jill looks over at me, still smiling.

My heart skips a few beats. "Exciting stuff," I remark.

"Next up, I've had Stevie prepare some ideas for the set. We're about ninety percent sure that we'll shoot in a semi-public setting. I've pulled some strings and lined up Jack Cleary's new restaurant as a potential venue."

Jack Cleary, isn't that—

"Ethan's mentor," Jill remarks under her breath. It's uncanny how she always seems to know what I'm thinking.

Claire smiles and nods. "He put in a good word for us. Plus, it'll generate buzz for the restaurant so it's a win-win. We're about to sign the contract."

"I'd like to see the place before you finalize," Gavin says. "Work out the logistics of setting up different cameras in there."

Claire agrees. The two of them talk amongst themselves for a little while, then Owen, the shrink, butts in with something else. I'm not really listening anymore and my mind starts to wander.

Looks like I'm getting a bit more responsibility on this project as well, just like Jill. After all, we're conducting the Glasgow audition.

Together.

On Saturday. The day after my postponed date.

Together.

Shit. I glance at her, battling butterflies in my stomach as I do. I'm going to spend the entire day and night in close proximity to her. While the day part is nothing new for us, it still concerns me. How on earth am I going to put her out of my head when she's going to be around constantly? And soon after that, Claire wants to start shooting the actual episodes, so we'll be working in close proximity yet again.

If I want this thing with Heather to work, I'm going to need a whole lot more self-control than I've been capable of these past couple of years. My plan of avoiding Jill altogether is obviously no longer viable.

CHAPTER EIGHT

* Jill *

Running into Damien at Claire's office was so weird. As if we're strangers, not best friends at all. One week and seemingly words apart. Although things seemed fine during the meeting, we hardly spoke. I asked about his date with Heather after—grudgingly, I might add—and he barely said a word.

The other thing that struck me was just how different he looked with the beginnings of a beard growing on his chin. So much more grown up and serious than before. Quite handsome…

And now, another five days later, we're going on a short trip together. Funny how life works sometimes.

I can only hope that we can get past whatever awkwardness has grown between us and find our way back to how things were. Claire, as well as our brand-new show, are depending on it. Plus, I still miss him. Desperately. No matter how many dreams I have about him, they're not enough to fill the hole his absence has left in my life.

Maybe I was right and Heather has convinced him to take a step back from our friendship? That would explain a lot. She's such a possessive cow.

It's five am when I arrive at Gatwick Airport. The self-check-in is quiet, and there's plenty of time to go for our boarding time, so it's no surprise that Damien isn't here yet.

Claire had told me to book a train rather than a flight, but I managed to find us a better deal; and despite the ungodly hour, I'm glad I did. Even if I'm already dreading the queue for the security check.

This short trip isn't going to be the relaxed getaway the two of us might need to fix our friendship, but it's better than nothing. And it's a huge deal, in career terms. For both of us.

It's just weird to think that by the end of today, we'll find ourselves in some fancy hotel together. All night, he'll be *right there*, with just a single wall separating us. And I'll be in my own bed, imagining all the crazy scenarios my subconscious has been feeding me about him lately.

Ever since coming back from the pub together, my fantasies have been out of control. Just this morning I woke up in the middle of a steamy make-out session with him. My skin is still tingling at the memory of it.

I'm still not sure if these dreams mean anything. Or am I just jealous now that he's back together with Heather? Maybe it's the whole dating show thing. Watching all the reality TV I can get my hands on in the name of research has made me realize what I'm missing in life. I want that same excitement. That passion, which seems to come so naturally for some people. Maybe Damien is just a convenient subject to latch onto, when I don't have anyone else in my immediate circle to fawn over.

These are the thoughts racing through my mind when I see him approach the spot near the self-check-in counters where I've chosen to wait. He's so tall. His head sticks out from the crowd as he approaches, even though he's slouching a little like he usually does. He doesn't like to stand out—that's why he chose a career in TV production rather than being in the limelight—but the sheer size of him makes that pretty much inevitable. And although I'm a little nervous, I do love how safe I feel once I spot him.

That end scene from *Love, Actually* is playing in my head, the one where Martine McCutcheon is running towards Hugh Grant at the airport and she jumps up into his outstretched arms… What would *that* be like? Damien could easily catch me, if only I'd be able to jump high enough.

"Well, last night was a shit show," Damien remarks, as he places his wheeled suitcase beside mine.

"Morning to you too," I reply. Trying to sound casual, when I feel anything but. There's a funny twinge in my chest where my heart should be. What happened last night?

"Yeah, morning, Jill," he says.

"Shit show, how?" I ask, looking up at him. He briefly makes eye contact with me, which gives me butterflies. Whoa. I don't think I've ever reacted to Damien quite like this. Maybe it's true what they say: distance does make the heart grow fonder. And his eyes. They're so… blue.

Oh, shut up!

"She stood me up. No call, no messages. Just radio silence. Again." He shrugs. "Please don't say you told me so."

I'm too shocked to say a word initially, but 'I told you so' isn't even in my top 100 of potential responses. Did their date last week go so badly that she opted out of the follow-up without any explanation? That's a pretty shitty thing to do. Despite initial impulses, I don't curse out the stupid cow like I really want to, but lead with compassion.

"Oh, no! That's terrible," I say, putting my hand on his arm. That simple gesture of closeness does something funny to the inside of my chest. He looks so upset. I wish I could help make it better.

Well, at least Heather is no longer a threat. Wait, *a threat?* What does *that* mean?

"That's it then. I tried. And I failed yet again."

"She didn't deserve you," I say. "You're better off." *Give me a chance and I'll never treat you like that.*

He looks at me skeptically. "I ought to just give

up. Guys like me don't stand a chance in hell. It's all about looks or money. And I have neither."

My heart contracts painfully. Now he's putting himself down and I hate it.

"Don't say that! You're a total catch. And the right woman will see that straightaway." *Fuck, I should have seen it years ago!*

He glumly shakes his head. "At this rate, I should sign myself up as a contestant on the show. At least I'd get a date out of it, even if it's a fake one. Anyway, how was your week?"

"Same old." Spent my Friday night at home by myself, counting down the minutes and seconds until I'd be here with him.

"Watched anything good on Netflix lately?" he asks.

He wouldn't need to ask if only we'd hung out with *each other* this past week. Like we used to.

Before I get the chance to answer, someone beckons us to our check-in counter. While they check our papers and weigh our bags, I'm still thinking of that airport scene. I'm Martine and Damien is Hugh Grant, only much, much taller and cuddlier.

I feel terrible that he's hurting this morning, and I'm even surprisingly bitter about—I'm not sure about what. But the underlying truth of the matter isn't lost on me. There's hope now. A glimmer of potential for the two of us. All I have to do is give him space to process what has happened, and *maybe* we'll be back to normal in no time.

* Damien *

Today was supposed to be different. Hell, last night was supposed to be different, and this morning I was supposed to still feel the high of a first date gone well.

Instead, I'm angry and disappointed for a multitude of reasons, some more obvious than others. I haven't slept, so my head hurts. And I hate airports at the best of times. The worst part is, in my eagerness to give Heather and me a chance, I may have ruined what I had with Jill.

So in short: I don't have a relationship with Heather, because she's vanished again without any explanation. And my interactions with Jill this morning are about as comfortable as a dentist's visit.

Although the brief contact of Jill's hand on my arm threatened to derail my entire thought process, I'm still not done obsessing about how last night went down. While the Ryan Air worker at the check-in desk checks and labels our luggage, I keep going over it again.

I never suspected anything when she postponed our date last week. So last night, I reached the restaurant a good fifteen minutes before our agreed time. I ordered a drink and settled in for a bit of a wait. After passing the time people-watching the other patrons, I started to get restless.

That's when I kept checking my phone. Refreshing our chat over and over, just so I wouldn't miss any message from her. Half an hour passed, and still, no message. I was starting to get flashbacks from two years ago.

The waiter brought me a menu, adding insult to injury, even though I'd told him already that I was waiting for someone else. I studied it anyway, just to pass the time, while wondering where Heather was. The story of her getting into an accident when we were first supposed to meet kept circling in my mind. Had something bad happened?

I tried to convince myself that I should keep an open mind. Maybe she's just not very punctual. Maybe her train got delayed. *Maybe…*

I waited for about an hour before concluding that maybe that old accident excuse was just that. An excuse.

In a perfect repeat of history, she never turned up, and I never got any message explaining why. She had no intention of ever meeting me. Not then, and certainly not now. But why? Why give me hope, only to let me down repeatedly?

"We ought to go to our gate," Jill tells me.

I try to snap out of it. "Right."

Dammit, why do I even care anymore? Why am I

giving a complete stranger so much power over my emotions? I got into this mess while trying to be proactive. The only way out that I can think of is to be proactive yet again. People can only take advantage of you if you let them.

I follow Jill through the crowds still waiting to check in and we soon join the queue at security. She makes a couple of attempts at conversation while we wait, but it's hopeless. I'm not in the mood. And she doesn't even look properly awake yet. So we just stand there in silence until it's our turn.

"Want to get some breakfast?" Jill asks once we make it to the other side of the X-ray machine.

"As long as it's liquid and caffeinated," I remark.

We find a small table outside a cafe near our gate and I watch while Jill takes her giant notepad out of the front pocket of her luggage and starts to read. She looks so thoughtful, the way she's crunching her eyebrows together while studying her notes. She's obviously taking this assignment extremely seriously.

As should I.

It's the first time either of us have been in charge of any part of a TV production. It's only auditions, which probably won't be shown on air in this case, but still. It's a big deal.

"It'll be fine, you know," I tell her.

She looks up at me and smiles. Despite everything, I feel a lot better just being around her.

BEST FRIENDS FOREVER

Maybe, just maybe, I'm not as broken up about Heather as I should be. I'm spending the weekend with my best friend. Despite the rough patch we've been going through, that's not so bad, is it?

"These are the applicants," she says, handing me a large stack of print-outs. "Provided they actually turn up."

"Right." I start leafing through the papers, which are individual application forms from dozens of people hoping to make it on the show. Some of the applications have headshots, others don't.

So weird. Blind dates are awkward enough, and yet there are all these people out there willing to go through that kind of torture on camera? People confuse me sometimes.

"Claire told me she wants people who are photogenic enough for TV, but still have that guy or gal next door vibe," Jill explains.

"Now there's an oxymoron."

"Right?"

Our drinks arrive and we both lean back in our seats, mugs in hand. I'm so eager to get some coffee into me that I almost burn my mouth with that first sip.

"Owen has prepared some questions to ask everyone, but Claire did say I can improvise if I want, so I added a few of my own." Jill pushes her notepad in my direction.

I pick it up and read it over. "Looks good to me."

"You really think so?" Jill looks up from her cup of tea with a concerned frown on her face. It's so cute how nervous she is about today. It's funny to me how she consistently underestimates herself.

"Claire wouldn't have given you this responsibility if she didn't think you could do it. You'll be perfect."

I lean across the table and put my hand on hers. God, that feels weird. Hot and cold at the same time, and absolutely nerve wracking. But seeing as she doesn't shy away from it, neither do I. And while we sit there like this for a few seconds, I make up my mind. As soon as I get a bit of privacy, I'm going to send Heather a message. One last one, in which I tell her it's over.

Because even if last night had gone according to plan, I still would have been here this morning. With my hand on top of Jill's and my heart racing out of control as a result. She might be way out of my league, but she's still the one for me. They say: 'it's better to have loved and lost than never to have loved at all'. The love has been there from the start. The loss is basically guaranteed.

Maybe one day I'll have the courage to test that theory properly. With Jill.

CHAPTER NINE

The short flight as well as our commute to the studio passes by in a blur. It doesn't take long for us to set up the space with a table and a couple of chairs for the two of us. Damien's small camera is setup on a tripod in between us, and another chair on the other side of the table is for the contestant.

It's super basic, but it'll do. The stage manager on staff got us a red backdrop to place behind the contestant's chair, as well as some studio lights, so the video quality should be good enough for social media promos or whatever else Claire wants.

Once the contestants start arriving, time flies even faster. We called them in batches, and seeing as it's just the two of us, we have our hands full trying to schedule everyone's five-minute-interview as well as record them all while keeping all the questions and observational notes straight.

So many faces eager to be on television; so little time. We've shortlisted half a dozen candidates already, rejected at least as many, and that's just before we break for lunch.

"Subway or KFC?" I ask Damien, who has been sitting beside me the entire time, simultaneously operating his camera as well as helping me keep the conversation with each potential contestant flowing.

He shrugs, but then gets distracted by something in the distance.

"Hi! Can I help you?" he calls out.

I lean over to follow his line of sight. Looks like someone has entered the studio, but he's partially obscured by the backdrop.

"Is this the dating show audition?" a male voice asks.

I can't get a good look at him, so I check my notes instead. One of the contestants from the previous time slot hadn't turned up. Perhaps this is him?

"Your name, please?" I say.

"Daniel," the man responds. "Please call me Dan."

"He's a bit late," Damien grumbles. "Interrupting our lunch break."

I leaf through my papers and find that he's the no-show from the earlier batch. I'm just about to tell him that he's missed his chance this morning, but then I spot the bright orange post-it on his application form. Owen was very keen on this guy for some reason, looking at the remarks he's scribbled on the file.

I show Damien the note, and he sighs and switches the camera back on.

Then I wave at Daniel to come closer. "You're a

little late, but I think we can fit you in. Please take a seat."

First impressions are… interesting. Dan reminds me a little of Damien. Though he looks to be a few years older and has a different hair color, as well as a beard, there's still some resemblance there. Along with the similarly solid build, I think it's the body language as well. Friendly but apprehensive. Like he's not really sure he wants to be here.

"I almost didn't turn up," Dan remarks with an awkward chuckle.

Damien gets up from his seat to give Dan a clip-on microphone while I observe the two of them. Yep, very similar indeed. He fits the guy-next-door part of the brief pretty well, but I don't know if he's going to be photogenic enough for Claire. Since he's Owen's pick, I'm inclined to shortlist him anyway and let the two of them fight it out later.

"Why didn't you want to come?" I ask once Dan's mic is on.

He smiles awkwardly. "Would you want to have a blind date on TV?" he counters.

I suppress a smile and glance at Damien, who looks equally amused. "I suppose not," I comment under my breath.

"It's a lonely world out there," Daniel remarks. "You guys are lucky to have each other, is all I'm saying."

Damien straightens his back. "Oh, we're not a couple!"

Dan raises both hands in defense. "Wow, okay. Sorry; I assumed."

I glance at Damien again, then back at Dan. Why do people keep thinking we're together? First Claire, and now this total stranger? Did the entire crew on *Decadent Desserts* think so too? Am I really that unaware of how people see us?

Damien is completely fixated on the preview screen on the camera and not making any eye contact with me. That was a pretty quick denial from his side, though. I'm surprised by how much the truth stings.

"Okay, well, why don't you tell me why you *do* want to be on the show, after thinking it over," I say.

Dan sighs and shakes his head. "I've come a long way these past five years."

"Right." I gesture at him to keep going.

"As you might have already gathered from my application, I've had some problems." Dan folds his arms in front of himself. Generally speaking, this kind of closed body language would be seen as a negative during an audition, but I'm keeping an open mind.

I quickly scan the first page of the questionnaire. Depression, obesity, social anxiety… *Okay.* I see where Owen is going with this one. He probably sees Dan as a challenge. If he can successfully use his metrics and tests to match up this guy, then he'll have proven himself and his system beyond any doubt.

"After spending all of my teens and twenties as a recluse, pretty much, I'm getting to a point in my life where I know I need to make some changes quickly. I've worked hard on myself, physically as well as mentally, so I hope that now I'm ready for the next step. I'm ready to find someone to share the rest of my life with."

"How much weight have you lost, exactly?" I ask.

"About two-hundred pounds."

Damien sits back and stares at Dan as well. "Wow."

"Right?" I whisper, pointing at the form in front of me. There are some other juicy bits in there which would play extremely well as an inspirational back-story. Though, he would need some training to improve his body language before we start shooting. I scribble down this observation on Dan's file.

"I know I haven't quite reached my goal yet." Dan gestures down at himself. He's definitely on the fluffy end of the scale still, but it must be mind-blowing to have gone through such a massive transformation.

"But, shit, I'm approaching thirty-five. If not now, then when? And I haven't had any luck dating on my own, so…"

I nod, then run through a few follow-up questions from Owen's notes. Dan's answers seem good enough, so there's nothing preventing me from adding his file to the stack of other potential candidates.

"Well," I start, "I would like to shortlist you. But you should know that there are very few spots available for this first season, so I can't promise anything right now. You'll hear back over the next week or so if you've made it onto the show."

Dan nods solemnly and starts to get up. "Thank you so much."

I can tell just from his expression and mannerisms that this audition was hard for him.

"All the best, Dan," I say.

We watch in silence as he unclips his microphone, sets it down on the chair, and says goodbye with an awkward little wave. Damien switches off the camera and leans back in his chair.

"That was different," he remarks.

"Right?"

"Claire won't like him."

I give him a suspicious side-eye. His observation isn't surprising. I don't think Claire will like him either, but there's something odd in Damien's tone when he says it. I would have thought that Damien of all people would be excited about having a more normal-looking guy on the show. There's always a certain type of person that applies to be on reality shows, and that can get old.

"Owen will veto her decision," I say. At least I hope he will.

He's so unlike the other contestants we've shortlisted today, and yet there's just something about him… He's suckered me right in, despite or maybe even because of his flaws.

"His episode is one I would love to watch. His back-story is great," I add.

"Uh huh."

"You don't agree?" I turn to Damien, studying his terse expression. I wonder what's gotten into him.

"I think if we put this guy on the show, our ratings will tank."

"Aw, why? People love a redemption story," I counter.

"Nobody wants to see a weird fat guy bumble his way through a blind date. Trust me."

I do. I desperately want to see this guy find happiness. In fact, I want it badly enough that I'd be willing to take on Claire if she disagrees.

Damien's words have struck a nerve in me, because they seem less about Dan and more about Damien's own bad experiences. And so I bite my tongue and let it go. This isn't the time to argue. Not when we're finally starting to work so well together.

Damien shakes his head and pushes his chair back. "So, Subway or KFC?"

***

By the time we're ready to head to our hotel, I'm exhausted, and I can tell Damien is too. That's what happens when you send two introverts to conduct auditions…

Once we're all checked in and heading upstairs with our limited luggage in tow, I can't help but wish that we could retreat to one room together. I could think of a number of ways to relax and unwind. Netflix and chill; yes, please! If only we were more than friends…

Even just to talk properly. Friendly conversation would be a vast improvement over the weird vibe that's been lingering between us these past couple of weeks and even part of the afternoon. Ever since Daniel's audition.

"Okay, I guess see you in the morning," he tells me, a bleak smile playing on his lips. He's tired too.

I want nothing more than to give him a hug. Tell him that everything is going to be okay. That he shouldn't feel so bad about what happened with Heather, because it's entirely her fault. But all of that would be weird and inappropriate.

"Breakfast at seven," I confirm, making a face to signal my displeasure at another early start.

He unlocks his room, and I unlock mine, a little

further down the hall. We're not quite next door to each other, but it's still the nearest we've ever spent the night. And my mind is reeling as a result. Until I push my door open and am greeted with a most unwelcome sight.

"Umm, Damien?" I call out across the hallway.

He rushes to my side and peeps through the open doorway with me. The entire room is flooded. The sound of water, gushing furiously, can be heard in the distance.

"Oh, balls," he says.

"I think I'm going to need a different room," I observe.

Like the gentleman that he is, he immediately takes charge and calls reception from his own room to explain the situation. Meanwhile, I wait outside the destroyed room, staring at the swimming pool inside like you would at a train wreck.

"Jill, there's another problem," Damien calls out to me.

"Oh, yeah?" I respond. *Of course there is.*

"Apparently they're fully booked due to some event this weekend. There's no other vacancy, so we'll just have to make do—"

I look at him for a second and press my lips together. It's a hopeless effort, because the first giggle erupts straightaway. It soon turns into an uncontrollable chuckle and then a laugh.

"What's funny?" he asks.

"Oh, I don't know!" I say.

Maybe it's the helpless look in his eyes. Or more likely, it's because only moments earlier I wished for the two of us to be sharing a room, and now my wish has come true.

It's probably because I'm exhausted, actually. This sort of thing does tend to happen to me at the most inopportune moments. I mumble something to that effect, while trying to get my inappropriate snickering under control.

"I could take the sofa," he suggests, after I follow him into his room.

I take one look at the tiny loveseat in the corner, and one look at Damien, with his six-foot-two and rather substantial frame, and shake my head while suppressing a further grin. "Don't be ridiculous."

"This is quite inconvenient," he complains. "Only one bed."

His remark stings, turning my mood more serious as well. I guess the reality of this situation is a lot more awkward than the fantasy.

"I'm really sorry to impose," I say. "You know what? I'll take the sofa. I can make it work."

"No, you're not! You're exhausted! I can't let you slum it on the sofa; that would be unacceptable."

This makes me smile yet again. It should be illegal to be this nice. Heather will never know what she's missing.

"So we'll share the bed, then. We're friends, right? We can handle it," I suggest. "They're twin mattresses and separate duvets anyway, so it shouldn't be a problem."

He looks at me funny for a moment, then looks at the huge bed and shrugs. "I'm okay with it if you are."

"I am." More than okay; I'm ecstatic. And at the same time, not okay at all. Tonight is going to be sweet, sweet torture.

"Do you want a shower now or in the morning? It would make sense to plan—" Damien stares at me rather than finish his sentence.

Yep, this is so weird already. All I can think about is Damien in the shower. With me. I wonder if we'd fit into the cubicle together. He *is* rather bulky, after all…

Stop fantasizing, dammit!

"It's up to you," I mumble.

To divert attention, I pick up my suitcase and put it on the still made up side of the bed. I try to look casual while I root around for my toothbrush and pajamas and neatly lay them out on the white sheets in front of me. The lacey blush pink shorts and matching strappy camisole look awfully skimpy under these new circumstances. As if I knew, subconsciously, what was going to happen. No, if I had known, I would have packed something a lot safer.

God, am I really going to wear this in front of Damien? Without a bra underneath? I steal a glance in his direction and notice his eyes on me already. His endlessly deep steel blue eyes. His stare gives me goose bumps.

This *is* inappropriate, isn't it?

"I think I'm going to have that shower now," he remarks, and rushes into the bathroom.

Awkward.

CHAPTER TEN

*** Damien ***

Jesus Christ. This trip, this entire weekend is testing every ounce of my self-control. Hence the smooth move I'd just pulled of fleeing into the bathroom. I'm such a chicken shit. What will happen once we actually have to lie down in the same bed together? How will I deal with *that?*

Only two weeks ago I'd promised myself to stay away from Jill to give Heather and me a good shot. Now that that's blown up in my face, I have no more reason to keep avoiding her, except…

Self-preservation.

It would be easy to give in to the temptation to let my imagination run wild, but soon enough reality will just kick me when I'm already down. Like right now, with both of us forced to share a room. The knowledge that she's right there, just on the other side of the bathroom door, hurts like nothing I have ever experienced before. Because a tiny part of me continues to have hope for us. It's that part I have to silence by any means necessary.

No matter what that guy at the audition assumed,

Jill and I could *never* be a couple. We're too mismatched. She's too capable and ambitious. Too beautiful. And I'm just not good enough to appear on her radar like that. Never have been. And so I've never even made an attempt to tell her.

What would *he* know about it, anyway? Someone who has never even gone on a single date in his life. That's why he's attempting to find love on a TV show of all things. What a joke.

I sigh deeply to try and get my frustration under control, but it doesn't work. As a result, I brush my teeth with a bit more vigor than necessary. Heart ache *and* bleeding gums? Why the hell not?

And why did Jill like him so much? What does *he* have that I don't? As far as I can tell, he's a basket case. Fine, a recovering basket case, but still. I can't recall ever feeling like this. Almost like I'm jealous. Of a complete stranger. It's laughable. Literally all that's happened is that Jill shortlisted him for our show. Nothing else, and I'm behaving like he tried to steal her away right from under my nose.

I put my toothbrush away again and check myself in the mirror while waiting for the water in the shower to warm up.

Was it the weight loss thing that impressed her? Losing two-hundred pounds is an achievement for sure. I can't beat that. I can't even seem to lose ten pounds, never mind more than that. But it's not like he's fit now. He looked about my size, maybe even slightly bigger.

He doesn't fit the image of what Jill likes at all. I don't get it.

After getting into the claustrophobia-inducingly small cabin, I close my eyes and let the warm water soothe my frazzled nerves. Still, I can't stop thinking about what happened during the audition.

She probably just likes the novelty of having him on as a contestant because it would make our show stand out from the competition. And despite not getting an assistant of her own due to budget constraints, Claire has entrusted a lot of the production work to Jill, like this trip. So this is a promotion for her, after all. She's likely going to be named in the credits alongside Claire and Owen.

Jill's career is important to her. That's why we get along so well, because I get it. Ours is a friendship of convenience. She needs someone to vent to who understands the long hours, the challenges of working on a tight schedule and being bound by confidentiality clauses, and other random crap this industry throws at you. Those things can make it hard to befriend normal people who work their regular nine-to-fives, five days a week with weekends off. So, why not latch on to someone on set for some companionship? Like me.

She has no idea what that does to me. To play the

reliable friend, when you so desperately want to be seen as something more. How could she know? I've done everything in my power to make sure she never finds out.

So, in a way, this is all my fault. This morning at the airport I briefly entertained the idea that I might take my shot and come clean to Jill. But, as soon as fate thrust the two of us together in the same room, I chicken out. Typical.

In the end, I spend ages in the shower ruminating about my friendship with Jill. I don't realize just how long it's been until I notice how spongy my hands and feet have become. And then I feel worse. Because it reminds me that by hogging the bathroom, on top of having inappropriate thoughts about her, I'm inconveniencing her as well.

So, I turn off the water, rush to towel myself off, get dressed, and grudgingly head back out. I'm still working through the residual guilt when it occurs to me that I haven't spared another thought for Heather all day. Despite the old heartache last night's disappointment dragged up, I've simply been too obsessed with Jill to care.

And so I take a deep breath, sit down on the bed, and do what I should have done in the first place. With my back still turned towards Jill, I type a quick message to Heather.

'Last night made me realize that we never had a

chance. We're over. Have a nice life.'

I don't know if I mean that last part, but hey.

Once I hit 'send' and put the phone on the bedside table, I do feel like a weight has been lifted off me. I'm lighter. Freer. I'm no longer the guy with the dangerous fascination with his friend and coworker, who's lying right there in the same bed. She's just a figment of my imagination, and not really here. It's just me, the TV, and my own stupid feelings. The soft breaths coming from her side of the bed are an illusion. The hints of her floral scent in the air are not real.

None of this is. It's all just a dream. A test of my resolve. The only choice I have is to make it through the night *somehow* without ruining everything we still have.

* Jill *

To avoid any further weirdness, I ended up changing into my pajamas while Damien had his shower, then got into bed and pulled the covers up right to my neck before he came back out.

He was right about one thing: I would have hated being stuck on the cramped sofa. The bed is great. The pillows are luxuriously plush, and the duvet is like a fluffy cloud on top of me. And the springy mattress is pure heaven, unlike the old lumpy one I have at home. I'm glad Damien was willing to share.

With all the lights off, the room is illuminated mostly by the flicker of the TV when Damien comes out of the bathroom, a significant while later. He looks so different now compared to how I get to see him normally. Dressed in a loose-fitting pair of shorts and a baggy t-shirt, he looks extra cuddly. It's extra sexy because of how casual it is. I don't think I've ever seen him wear shorts before, only jeans and cargo pants, so this feels like a rare treat.

Repeating my mantra from last week, I try to steer the course.

Don't get aroused...

It's kind of too late for that, ever since I started imagining him naked earlier, but maybe I can dial it back in. The last thing I need is to have one of my sexy dreams, with him lying right there beside me!

I hold my breath and pretend not to watch his every move while he sits down on his side of the bed. The mattress dips down luxuriously underneath him, while he pauses there for a minute, checking his phone. Since it's a twin, I can't feel his movements, I can only imagine them. I can also imagine rolling over and ending up right next to him in that dip, with my head resting against his shoulder.

What would it feel like to lie next to him, cuddled up in his arms? What would his body feel like against mine? It'd be so much more intimate than when we cuddled in the back of the Uber. And how would things progress from there? Quickly, if I had my way. These are dangerous thoughts, which I'd be better off barring from my mind again.

Do not get aroused!

We won't be cuddling tonight. But now that we're sharing a room, I wonder if we'll chat before we go to sleep. I have to think back to what he told me this morning at the airport. Will he bring up Heather? He also said that guys like him don't stand a chance on the dating scene. What will I say to make him feel better about it? It's a fine line to tread, and now that we're lying in bed together… Certain boundaries are already eroding, at least at my end.

I hate that he's so hard on himself, when I've come to realize that I love everything about him. To me, he's perfect, but I don't know how to tell him that without making things weird between us. We're colleagues as well, after all. If I remember our latest mandatory sexual harassment seminar properly, telling a colleague how attracted you are to them is frowned upon.

And anyway, he doesn't like me like that.

"What are you watching?" he asks.

"Not sure; some shitty disaster movie. I just switched it on, but I think I dozed off shortly after," I lie.

I didn't sleep, though I still have no idea what

happened on screen. There's no way I'll relax any time soon; a part of me is still obsessing about Damien getting soaped up in the shower... *Oh, shut up!*

I turn onto my side, facing him, and study his features in the blue flicker of the TV. He looks tense, with deep creases forming on his forehead. So serious. So handsome.

"Thanks so much for letting me stay in your room," I whisper.

"Oh come on! Where else were you going to go, the hallway?" he says, closing his eyes.

"Still...Hey, if you're not in a mood to watch TV either, we can just turn it off."

"Yeah, sure."

I pick up the remote and turn it off, plunging us a little further into darkness. It takes a moment for my eyes to adjust to the dim glow of the nightlight in the corner.

He changes position slightly and snuggles into the pillow, but the creases on his face don't disappear. I wonder what he's thinking about. About Heather and the date that never happened? Whatever it is, I tend to believe it's best to talk things through.

"Hey..." I start.

"Hm?"

"What happened last night?"

He sighs. "Exactly the same thing as two years

ago."

I frown and shake my head. "Well, how did your first date go last weekend? It's odd for someone to just vanish before the second one."

He turns and faces me with a dejected look on his face. "I never told you, did I?"

I shake my head. We barely spoke at all this past week. God, it hurts to be left out of the loop.

"Something came up at the last minute, so we postponed our plan. Yesterday was still technically supposed to be our first date."

I'm speechless. That's a pretty big thing to keep from me. I remember the suspicions I had the last time we discussed her. About her being a catfish. It would explain a lot.

"Who for?"

"What?"

"Did something come up for you or for her?" I ask, though I don't even know why I'm trying to analyze this. He's been going through all this shit, and I never even knew. Maybe we aren't as close as I had wanted to believe. But why? What happened?

"Just forget it. It's over and done with." With those two short sentences and a shake of his head, he ends our conversation.

Just as well, because I don't know what to think anymore. Who even is he? Who are we to each other?

I run through every single one of his words again

and again. Heather was a no-show. I'm sure she was the reason they postponed, because there's no way Damien would have. He's pretty dependable otherwise.

That's three strikes against her. The whole situation stinks. I guess I was right about her.

"Good night," he mumbles after a lengthy silence.

"'Night."

I lie still on my side of the bed, hyper aware of every sound in the room. His breaths; a bit on the faster side compared to normal. The occasional rustle of the sheets. The sound of the mattress shifting when he turns onto his side, away from me. And the relentless beat of my own heart, reminding me that I'm not going to find any rest tonight. Because whatever is going on with him, with *us*, it bloody hurts.

I thought we were better than this. That we wouldn't let anything get in between us long term. Not a dumb drunken conversation, and not an online girlfriend who turned out to be a bitch. But instead of letting me in, he's locking me out.

Maybe he's just too upset. Maybe I'm expecting too much.

Once it gets quiet enough for me to suspect he might have fallen asleep, I can finally breathe again. Then, I leave the safety of my bed to take my turn in the bathroom.

CHAPTER ELEVEN

*** Damien ***

It's two am when I finally give up on trying to sleep and pick up my phone. With my back turned towards Jill and the brightness set to low, I hope I don't end up waking her. This is literally the only thing I can think to do, because the alternative is to let my mind wander some more. And I just can't take it anymore.

Just the sound of her soft breaths, a couple of feet away from me, is doing my head in. And although I've made sure to have my back turned throughout, I can still *see* her. I can still imagine her in that little outfit she unpacked earlier before I'd gone to the bathroom.

Jesus Christ. What am I supposed to do with mental images like that?

For now, it's doom scrolling to the rescue. Facebook, Instagram, anything I can get my hands on. But it's all just superficial and boring. None of it works to put out the fire in my heart.

What does she look like underneath the cover? Wearing that frilly little top with the thinnest spaghetti straps I've ever seen, and even tinier shorts underneath?

Thankfully I didn't *see* her in it. Yet. Or I would have lost my mind by now. And with it, the last remnants of my self-respect. Tonight I could still pretend that I'm broken up about Heather and hence avoiding any real conversation.

But what will happen in the morning? Sooner or later, we'll both have to get up and get ready. *And then…*

And then the game will be up. I will reveal myself as the creepy pervert I am, fantasizing about my friend and coworker's half-naked body the whole damn night. And I'll still have the boner to prove it.

I should be ashamed of myself.

She'd look smoking hot in those pajamas, though. I'm sure of it.

I force a deep breath to rid myself of all these demons. Sexy, seductive demons that seek to convince me that just one little fantasy won't harm anyone. Just for a minute. Just this once. I must give in, work through it, and get it out of my system.

But I just can't reconcile that idea with the fact that I actually care about her, deeply. This isn't some momentary attraction. I *love* her. More than I've ever loved another human being. It hurts to admit it, but it's the truth.

I would do anything for her. Except, apparently, stop lusting after her and defiling her in my mind.

Anything but that.

My wrist grows sore from holding the phone at this strange angle, and my thumb gets weary of scrolling endlessly through my newsfeed, yet I still can't find any peace.

You know what you need? That bad little voice in my head starts to speak. *You need to blow off some steam!*

Fuck. No, I don't.

Yes, if you do that, you'll be able to fall asleep and get through the rest of the night without making a fool of yourself!

As wrong as the thought is, there's a core of truth to it, and I know it. And there's absolutely no point in arguing about it.

My fantasies are my own, aren't they? Private. Secret. As long as she never finds out, it can't hurt her.

A moment later, I finally give in to that as well. I get up as quietly as I can manage, grab my phone as a makeshift torch, and head back to the safety of the en-suite bathroom. Before closing the door behind me, I look back once. Although it's dark, I can just about make out Jill's face, snuggled into her pillow, with her medium-length blonde hair framing her relaxed features. While I'm in turmoil, she's fast asleep. Good. That way she'll never know what I'm about to do.

* Jill *

I keep on staring at the dark ceiling, waiting for Damien to come back. Why? Not sure. He's a grown man; it's up to him how much time to spend in the bathroom. It has been a *very* long time, though. At least half an hour. Or does it just seem that way?

I turn over and check my phone. It's nearly three.

I hope he's alright…

Another few minutes pass. All this while, there has been no sound coming from the bathroom. What is he up to?

Finally, I swing my legs over the edge of the bed and get up. The plush carpet feels inviting underfoot, so I don't even bother to wear my slippers.

I carefully shuffle forward, towards the thin sliver of light emanating from underneath the bathroom door, and hold my breath to listen. It's completely quiet inside.

My knock on the door pierces the silence.

"Umm… Damien? Are you okay?"

Now there's a sound inside. A clatter, like something plastic has fallen down and hit the hard tile, followed by his muffled voice.

"Yeah. Fine," he says.

"Are you sure? I woke up a while ago and you were gone…" I bite my bottom lip. I can't very well tell him I've been up all night obsessing about him, can I?

"I'm good. Go back to bed."

I close my eyes and take a deep breath. "If something's wrong, you can tell me." *You've been in there for at least forty minutes already, if not more!* I clear my throat. "You're not sick, are you? I packed medicine."

"No, no. It's nothing."

There's something in his tone—a slight tremble in his voice—which convinces me he's lying. He doesn't sound like himself. I can't shake it. My frustration from earlier vanishes, only to be replaced with concern. I need to make sure he's fine. I need to *see* him.

"Okay, but… I kind of need the toilet as well," I confess. "So, whenever you're done…"

He mutters something, probably a curse. A few moments later, the door finally unlocks.

I feel weak with nerves as I wait a few steps away from the door to give him room. He doesn't really look at me when he emerges. Not at my face, anyway. His eyes do seem to linger momentarily… on my chest.

It occurs to me that this is the first time he's seen me dressed like this. That is to say, not dressed much at all, in this revealing little frilly cami and shorts set. When I first wore it, I'd hidden myself away under the duvet… I was so worried about my outfit that I only got out of bed in the dark. While he had his back turned.

And now I've been inconveniently lit up by the bathroom lights and on full display. Awkward.

"Are you sure you're okay?" I ask.

He pauses, giving me time to look at him more closely. Those same creases on his forehead which I'd noticed earlier in the evening are still there. In fact, they've been etched into his features even deeper.

Just as he walks away from me, towards the bed, he finally answers. "No, not really."

Worried, I pivot and approach his side of the bed instead of heading into the bathroom like I'd planned.

"Hey, what's wrong?" I ask.

He shakes his head and sits down with his arms folded and head hanging low.

"Can't sleep."

"Are you sure you haven't caught something?"

"No."

What on earth has gotten into him? He's been acting weird anyway, but his answers have become monosyllabic now. At least earlier he was still speaking in whole sentences. The whole Heather situation must really be weighing on his mind.

"Well, at least try to rest for a while. Another long day tomorrow," I say.

Finally, he looks up at me with a pained expression on his face. "I can't do this. Not with you here."

That's not what I thought he would say. Not

Heather, then…

"I'm not sure I understand," I whisper. My heart is beating so loudly I'm sure even he can hear it.

"Just… forget I said anything," he grumbles. He gets up off the bed and takes a seat next to his suitcase on the little sofa.

Something else is troubling him, and I don't know what to do or say. He doesn't like me being here, that much is clear. But where would I go? What have I done to annoy him, knowingly or unknowingly?

"Look, I'm really sorry," I say.

"You have nothing to be sorry about." He folds his arms and stares at his feet. This is pretty much the body language Daniel displayed during his audition earlier. The same nervous energy. The similarities are uncanny. But we're friends, not strangers. Doesn't he know he can tell me anything?

Instead, he looks super uncomfortable, and I tense up further as a result.

"I could check with reception if perhaps something else has opened up? Maybe a guest who never turned up?" I suggest.

He shakes his head. "Go to sleep. Just let me sit here for a while."

"Yeah, as if," I mutter under my breath.

"Hm?"

"I haven't slept a wink all night either," I confess, sitting down on my side of the bed and staring down at the floor. Realizing just how much leg I have on display right now, I pick up a corner of the duvet and drag it across my lap.

"Look, I'm sorry this is weirding you out. I didn't think—" He stops talking, and just looks at me funny for a moment. If this was any other guy, under any other circumstances, I'd be wondering if he's checking me out. But that can't be, can it?

"It's not. I mean, it wasn't," I whisper.

"But it is now, huh?"

"You're acting strangely, so… yeah," I mumble. "If you'd tell me what's bothering you exactly, perhaps I could help." My emotions are all over the place now. Whatever this is, I just want to talk through it. If we don't, how will we ever get back to normal?

He lets out an exasperated scoff. "Yeah, no chance."

His outright refusal hurts, so I retaliate without hesitation. "Right, sorry I cared."

He sighs again and shakes his head. "No, I should apologize. I didn't mean to be gruff," he says.

"Then why don't you just come out and tell me what's on your mind?" I insist. "Let's put the topic to bed at least, even if we won't be able to sleep ourselves. Did I do something to piss you off?"

"Alright, you know what? Only because you're being so persistent." He sounds annoyed too now.

"Okay!" I realize that this is turning into an argument, but at least I'm going to get the truth.

"Okay!" he repeats, then clears his throat. "I can't stand being in the same room with you right now."

I frown and try not to let his non-answer anger me further. *Thanks, Captain Obvious!* "Again, why? What'd I do?"

"Nothing! You did absolutely nothing. You're being your own perfect self, and I'm… God forgive me for what I'm about to say."

"Just bloody say it! We'll worry about God later."

He groans in frustration. "Every time I look at you. Every time I close my eyes. Every time I hear you breathe in the dark. Or whenever the sheets rustle beside me. Every time I catch your scent in the air—" He gestures wildly with his hands, but the words aren't coming anymore. Again, with any other guy, under any other circumstances, I'd know where this is going… But this is *Damien!* It doesn't compute.

"What?" I whisper.

"I want things. I want unspeakable things! But we're just friends. And it fucking hurts just to be here right now. With you."

I feel my mouth opening, and closing, without any sound coming out. I'm not even sure I'm breathing anymore. Holy shit balls.

"I'm sorry! I didn't want to say anything because I knew it'd ruin our friendship. But I just can't—" he rants. "I couldn't stand to be in that bed for a second longer, with you right next to me! …And now you're staring at me. You're taking it badly. Fuck, I'm such a moron!"

I'm feeling lightheaded, floaty. Am I dreaming? Surely, I fell asleep and this is all just the beginning of an epic wet dream. I hope I'll remember it come morning, because it's bound to be a good one.

"I'm so sorry, Jill," he whispers. "I shouldn't have said anything."

I shake my head. Damn, I never expected this!

"I'm speechless," I say.

"Yeah. I can see that." He rests his head in his hands. And although I want nothing more than to go over to him and tell him it's alright, I just can't move. My feet are glued to the carpet, and at some point I started white-knuckling the duvet in my lap.

The only thing that does move is the corner of my mouth. It flutters and tickles and turns into a smile. And once I'm grinning like an idiot, the rest of my body follows. First with a singular chuckle, then a giggle, until I can't contain my laughter anymore, such is the tension I feel. If I don't let it out, I might just explode. After all the doubts I had all night. All the fear I felt, thinking that he was angry with me! And the heartache I imagined him going through because of his failed date with Heather…

I couldn't have been more wrong.

"Great," he grumbles. "That's what I get for baring my soul."

I can't speak anymore, I'm wheezing so hard.

"Screw you, Jill."

The foul look he gives only makes me laugh more. Oh shit. He must think I've lost my mind.

"I'm sorry!" I pant.

"I don't know what I was expecting, but I didn't think you'd laugh at me. Anyone else, sure. But not you."

I choke on my own breath once, then do everything I can to swallow my laughter for a moment just to be able to get a few words out.

"I'm not!" I protest. "Not laughing at you!" At myself, more like. At being such an idiot, I didn't even see the writing on the wall when it might as well have been lit up in neon all this time.

"Right. Yes, you are!"

Tears are streaming down my face, and I'm starting to tremble all over. Oh shit, this is bad. Of course he's furious. How would I feel if someone burst out laughing after a confession like that?

"Damien. Please. I would never—"

"Save it. Go to bed. I need some air."

He gets up off the sofa and starts walking towards the door. That finally makes me stop, as a fresh surge of blind panic builds up inside me. Now I've done it.

I've not just ruined the moment, I've obliterated it.

"Damien!" I call out. "Wait! Don't go!"

CHAPTER TWELVE

*** Damien ***

"Wait! Don't go!" she calls after me.

But I don't listen. I just keep heading for the door, determined to get the hell out of there before I fall apart.

In my time of weakness, when Jill interrupted what was supposed to be a moment of solitude in the bathroom, I gave myself away. I told her the one thing I vowed I would never confess to.

I told her how I really feel.

Knowing how this would end. Knowing that it couldn't possibly work out. *Stupid, stupid, stupid!*

My fingers are trembling as I try to open the door, which delays me. That's when she catches up behind me.

"Damien, come on. Hear me out at least."

Her hand lands on my arm, but I shake it off immediately. That's how intensely it burns. My heart can't take any more of this. Not right now. I know it was dumb to tell her the truth, but I never expected to be mocked for it.

"I think I've heard enough," I say.

"Damien, you're my favorite person in the whole world," she counters.

God, that hurts even more. Fucking am I? If this is how she treats her so-called favorite person, then I pity anyone who falls out of favor with her.

"Come on, you know how I get! Always reacting in the worst possible way. I can't help it, especially when I'm tired! And I haven't slept all night either. Please don't take it personally!" she pleads.

I take a deep breath before responding in as calm a tone as I can manage. "It's a bit difficult not to take this personally, given the very personal circumstances."

"Damien, I love you." She tries to touch my arm again.

Her words, as well as the gesture she chose to combine them with, hit me like a dagger through the heart. This time I'm too weak to do anything about it, so I just end up staring at her hand on me.

"Sure. As a friend," I grumble, glancing at her face.

She looks sincere, kind of. If it wasn't for the tears still staining her face, obvious evidence of how hard my admission made her laugh.

"God, Damien! Don't you understand? I couldn't sleep all night because I was going crazy too!" she adds in a low whisper.

I sigh and try to rationalize what she's telling me. "It is a weird situation. Like we've crossed a line without even doing anything. I don't know how to take it back."

"No, no! I was going crazy because I wanted so badly to cross *all the lines.*"

Hard as I try to understand, now her words stop making sense altogether.

"What?"

I keep staring at her, and she keeps looking up at me with an odd frown on her face. It's an expression I don't think I've ever seen on her before. Fear mixed with… hope?

"Ever since the farewell party," she explains, "I've come to realize that maybe I never wanted to be just friends with you. That there was always something else there. I was just too stupid and ignorant to identify it properly, but—"

"You… Oh my *God!*" I exhale sharply and shake my head.

"But you never showed any interest in me, never so much as asked me out. So I kept quiet. And then of course you started talking to Heather again, so…"

"You're joking, right? You've got to be fucking joking."

"As if I'd ever joke about something like this!" she hisses.

"But… I've seen the sort of guys you go out with," I stammer. "And you never said anything either!"

"You've seen *one* guy I've gone out with. And I broke it off with Frank a month after meeting you." She chews on her bottom lip before continuing in a low whisper. "In part, *because* of meeting you."

I can feel my eyes widen as the wind is knocked out of my chest. I simply must be dreaming. None of this is making any sense. From her ex, Frank, to her superhero crush, Thor. She's attracted to big, muscular Viking-looking dudes. Not me. *Never* me. So, how could she possibly be telling me the truth?

"The more time I spent around you, the more I realized that what I had with Frank just wasn't—" She sighs deeply and shrugs. "It didn't feel right. Not like how I feel when I'm with you. Plus, he was a bit of a dick, as you know. Any time I had the choice between going on a date with him or hanging out with you, I chose you."

"Jesus," I mumble.

"So you see…" Her voice trails off.

"This is just a dream, isn't it?"

"I should fucking hope not!"

I stare at her. Although the room is still kind of dark, I can see so much in her that I've never seen before. Maybe it's my mind playing tricks on me, trying to attach even more meaning to this moment than there already is. The honesty in her eyes. The creases of worry on her forehead. The slight gleam that has returned to her brown eyes during her own confession… The soft tremble in her chest whenever she exhales. She looks so fragile, and infinitely more beautiful for it. And thanks to that tiny little outfit she has on, she also looks super hot. If I didn't know better, I'd wonder if I was even awake right now. Maybe I slipped in the bathroom and hit my head, and this is all a comatose dream.

"Jill. I swear to you, if you're just trying to make me feel better and you don't really mean it…"

"I mean every word."

"It'll break me, Jill." I can barely breathe anymore, especially not while looking at her. At her petite body, with curves in all the right places, barely contained within the little strappy top and short-shorts. Or at the sincerity in her eyes. I can't decide which is more addictive.

"Right back at ya," she whispers.

We're both silent for a painful few seconds, standing only a foot or so apart, with her hand resting on my arm. I glance down at it before locking onto her eyes again. I take a deep breath to calm myself, but all that does is overwhelm my senses with her sweet perfume.

"Now what?" I wonder aloud.

"Now, you kiss me. Or we forget we ever had this conversation. Your choice."

* Jill *

My throat closes up as soon as I challenge him to kiss me. Not sure where all this assertiveness is coming from, but I do know one thing. There's no turning back. We can't be friends anymore. Tonight, we've opened Pandora's box of messy emotions once and for all. And the past is just that, lost in time forever.

He presses his lips together and takes a deep breath, then he rests his hand on my cheek. I close my eyes and lean into it, into him. So warm. So inviting.

"You're so beautiful, Jill. And I'm—" His breath is ragged when he inhales deeply.

I open my eyes just in time to see him shake his head in shock.

"Kiss me before I lose my mind," I beg.

I'm quite a bit shorter than he is, obviously. If I pretended like that never factored into my attraction, I'd be lying. I love having to look up to him when we talk. I could climb this man like a tree and be the happiest girl in the world. To think that I might get to do that now blows my mind. The singular regret I have in all of this is that I didn't stop to think about it before. I could have saved both of us from a world of pain. That whole Heather episode never needed to happen.

He leans down, and his other hand ends up on the small of my back. It makes me giddy. I take a deep breath, just to get my heart rate under control, but it's pointless. His scent fills my lungs and throws me off balance all over again. A mixture of soap, toothpaste, cologne. He smells amazing. Even better than normal.

I wrap my arms around his neck and carry on staring into his pale blue eyes. They seem to sparkle a little, even in the half-dark. There's so much warmth in them and such kindness.

"Jill," he whispers.

I always knew he was a good man, the best. A genuinely nice guy, who just hadn't gotten the chance to show that part of himself to another person, at least not for as long as I've known him. I'm glad for that now. Selfishly, because I've always wanted it all for myself. And seeing him give his heart to someone else would have broken me.

That's why I was so distrustful of Heather. It makes perfect sense now. I was deeply jealous of what they could have become. Her loss is my gain.

"Yes?" I hear myself answer.

He leans in closer, and our noses brush past each other. My lips are so close to his, I can almost taste him. His eyes snap shut, and he's frozen in place. Hot breaths tickle my face. I can't stand the tension anymore and bridge the last remaining gap myself, tentatively pressing my lips against his for our first kiss.

It's so beautiful, it brings fresh tears to my eyes. How I've dreamed of this moment. During those times when the thought of him infiltrated my dreams, I always rejected it as just an innocent fantasy or simple biology, but now I know it was so much deeper. What an idiot I have been.

I've loved Damien for two years now. I was just too stupid to realize it.

His lips are soft, gentle, just like the rest of him. But that's only at first. His kisses turn firmer almost straightaway. Slow, almost hesitant exploration turns a lot more deliberate. More eager. I can't stop, and it seems, neither can he. It's as if this first contact has opened up a new world for us. A whole new language to express ourselves. One that doesn't need words anymore. We need not ask for permission; we just do whatever feels right.

He straightens himself, and I tighten my grip around his shoulders, raising myself up just a little. His arms wrap around me, and I find myself suspended in the air. I try to hook my legs around his waist, but it's kind of a lost battle, because I can't quite reach. He holds me tight in his embrace and safely carries me through the dark room until we reach the bed. There, he lays me down gently on my back, and tries to back away, but I won't let him.

I continue to cling onto Damien with all my

strength. I carry on loving his mouth with mine, drinking in his scent, trying to memorize how his tongue curls around mine, as if to tell me that I've been his for years.

I adore how his body feels, crushing against me, causing me to sink deeply into the luxurious mattress. I can sense him surrender to me now. The tension in his back releases little by little. No longer is he trying to retreat, but instead he melts down on top of me, transferring most of his weight onto his elbows, all the while kissing me like I've never been kissed in my entire life.

Two years have passed since the start of our friendship. Two years of emotions, doubts, uncertainty, and unrequited longing culminate in this moment. Because I understand that everything he's unleashing on me isn't just a passing fad or mild curiosity from his side. It's so much deeper.

Whereas I was too dumb to see that the perfect guy was right in front of me all this time, he knew his heart all along. And he's suffered as a result. I can put it together now. All those days spent on set, shooting various projects alongside each other. How I'd always feel his eyes on me no matter what we were doing. How it would comfort me to know he was looking out for me.

For him it wasn't a comfort. It was a compulsion. An obsession.I was the luckiest girl in the world without even knowing it. But now I do.

I can't decide where to touch him first. His face, his closely cropped hair which feels so nice brushing against my palm… I quickly carry on downwards, feeling his broad shoulders through the thin cotton of his t-shirt. I love how big he is and how petite and fragile he makes me feel, which, admittedly, at five foot three, I pretty much am. More than anything, I love how cuddly he is. Frank wasn't, of course, as Damien already pointed out to me. The two are polar opposites, which might be what I like best about him. Damien is different. Unique. Safe. Perfect. An entirely new chapter in my life.

Mine.

He tenses again when I slip my hand underneath his shirt and touch the bare skin of his back for the first time. So seductively soft and smooth. I can't get enough. As soon as I dig my fingers into his flesh just a bit more firmly, he lets out a low growl and pulls away from our kiss, only to move downward, planting his lips onto the side of my neck.

"I had no idea," he half-whispers. His voice is deeper than normal. His words tickle and give me goose bumps.

"Me neither."

"I can't believe you're letting me do all this."

I buck my hips upwards. "You can do whatever you want with me."

He groans into my neck, then bites down on it, just a little. Enough to make me squirm.

Under any other circumstances, with any other guy, this would be so weird. I've never been quick to give it up; I've never fallen into bed with someone moments after a first kiss. But Damien isn't just any guy. I know him better than anyone.

We've had plenty of foreplay to get us here, in every daydream I've had and countless nighttime ones as well. And now… Everything I've fantasized about is about to come true.

Okay, you can get horny now.

And there's no doubt in my mind that we're exactly on the same page. I can feel his need for me in everything he does. In every ragged breath that leaves his body and caresses my skin. I can sense how he's losing his focus ever so slightly as he runs his hand up my side, sliding underneath the satiny fabric of my camisole for the first time. A subtle twitch, like a micro expression. It may be easy to miss by the casual observer, but it's obvious to me now.

Because I *know* him. I feel what he feels. I want what he wants.

I've never seen him like this before, except in my dreams, and even then it didn't quite match up to reality. But if my own arousal is any indication, he's sure to be absolutely desperate as well.

Most of him is soft to the touch; my Damien

definitely isn't sculpted or muscular in any way, but with one notable exception. Right there in his shorts, there's one part of him that's rock solid, and prodding persistently into my thigh. It drives me crazy to know how ready he is for what's to come. He's waited for years, but now the goal is in sight.

His hand burns into my bare skin. I wish he'd go further right away, such is my impatience. I want his hands on my breasts and his lips kissing every inch of me, including those most intimate places which haven't been touched by another person in two whole years.

Ever since Frank, I've going through a dry spell. Knowingly or unknowingly, I've been holding out for this very moment. And I'm so grateful that I have. Anything less would have been a disappointment. No one else can ever compare.

"Jill…" The way he whispers my name makes me squirm again. "Stop me."

"No."

"Stop me, before I'm unable to." His voice sounds pained. Why does he protest so much?

CHAPTER THIRTEEN

*** Damien ***

"Stop me before I'm unable to," I plead.

"Never," Jill says.

"Baby, please," I beg. Not sure what I'm begging for, since I already have her permission. For whatever. But my mind seems to have trouble getting out of its own way.

"I want you." She reaches down as far as she can and grabs a handful of my ass.

It feels… It feels new. Powerful. A little awkward, and yet so hot I can't resist anymore.

A moan escapes my lips as I grind into her. How small she feels underneath me. Funny.

So small and seemingly fragile, when she's actually the strongest person I know.

I'm so hard it hurts. It's probably uncomfortable for her on the receiving end too.

She wiggles underneath me, wedging her hand in between us and finally reaching my package after a short struggle. As soon as her fingers close around my hard length, I lose all control.

"Oh God, Jill!" I call out.

She raises her hips in my direction and tightly wraps her other arm around my neck, forcing my face down against hers for more feverish kisses. If there was any doubt left in my heart that she truly wants this, it's wiped away now.

Instead, I'm filled with a new fear. We've been working up to this moment for so long, spending years in denial or misunderstanding of each other's motives, as well as our own. *What if…*

What if I don't measure up? What if I disappoint her?

"I need you," she whispers, in between kisses. "Damien, I've never wanted anything more!"

I freeze, just for a moment. But that's enough for her to pick up on my trepidation.

"What's wrong?" she asks, loosening her grip on my neck. "Do you not want this?"

I shudder my hips into her hand. Her touch feels so good. Her entire body feels so good. I just have to… Dammit, I have to focus!

"Promise me you won't regret it in the morning," I say.

"I would never. You?" she counters.

"Jesus, no!" Although I'm still struggling to get my head right, my body is carrying on with a mind of its own. My hips continue to move, rutting into her. With only her hand and a thin layer of fabric keeping our bodies from joining, I really can't hope to fight instinct any longer.

"Take me, then!" she demands.

Fuck. Has any man ever been able to resist an invitation like that? Especially coming from the woman of his dreams? I think not!

Although she's been trapped underneath me ever since I got on top, she manages to wriggle her thighs free, spreading them wide. Then she fumbles with my shorts and her own, releasing my previously trapped erection, and guiding it where it needs to go.

It happens so quickly, I don't get the chance to over think it. Soon, I feel my tip touching her warmth. She's wet and inviting. I get up onto my elbows and just look at her. At her pretty face; greedy eyes; moist, parted lips… This is what perfection looks like.

"It's all for you," she breathes.

Is it? Is it really?

A part of me is still expecting to wake up from this dream. But it's too intense to be one. Too real. And I've never felt a more urgent need to seize the moment than I do right now.

Because I'm starting to believe her. For the first time since all of this unfolded, now I look into her warm amber eyes and I can clearly see that she's been telling me the truth. There's no acting involved here. She's not just playing along to make me happy. She *wants* this. *Me.*

And it's my duty as a man—*her man*—to give it to her. I already know I'd give her anything, my own life included. The fact that she's asking me for my body isn't much of a sacrifice. I've been fantasizing about this moment for years.

So, I push through what's left of my self-doubt and into her. Slowly, edging forward, until little by little, she surrounds me and I am home.

That's what it feels like. After two years of yearning, I've finally arrived exactly where I'm meant to be. And the end result is my complete surrender and salvation.

The tension I felt all night releases, and I feel lighter than I ever have. No longer am I burdened by self-doubt. This is it. My one shot, and I'm taking it.

Searing heat fills my chest, burning up the overload of butterflies that had collected in there before. No more nerves. No more hesitation. Everything I'm doing, everything I am, for the first time in my life it's all *right*. In the right place, at the right time, with the right person.

"You okay?" I whisper. "I'm not hurting you, am I?"

She shakes her head and smiles. "You're perfect. Don't stop!"

As Jill coaxes me into speeding up my rhythm, I do my best to comply. I want to give her everything she needs. Anything. Anytime.

God, she's tight.

If this is how she wants it, I want nothing more. Who I thought I was, what I thought I deserved or indeed, didn't deserve in life, no longer concerns me. Every single thing I am, I owe to her. My life, my heart, my everything… it's hers.

She mumbles something I can't hear, then holds on tight to my neck. Whatever it is, her urgent tone is enough to pull me closer to the edge… which is something I had hoped to avoid, at least for a while. But then, I'm over the edge and there's nothing else I can do but grit my teeth and groan.

Dammit, my mind isn't even in control anymore! My body moves back and forth on its own while she continues to tilt her hips up into me, trying to match my feverish pace.

Until I freeze.

Every single one of my muscles tenses and my movements grind to a halt.

"Oh fuck," I grunt.

"Damien! Don't stop!" she whines. I open my eyes and see the desperate look in her eyes. And although it's the hardest thing I've ever done, I overcome the rigidity in my limbs and start to move again. Through my own release. Through the overwhelm of my own orgasm. I keep pushing, again and again, plunging into her tight, hot depths, until her eyes roll back and her motor control starts to falter. Fingernails dig deeply into the flesh on my back, signaling that I have succeeded.

Sweet relief. I didn't know I had it in me.

She whimpers my name as her pussy contracts around me. I can actually feel it! How bizarre. This has literally never happened to me before. I'm not the most experienced guy, but still. Never have I ever felt anything like this.

I did this. I might be an awkward nerd most of the time, but I still made her cum. During our first time, with so much riding on it. Unbelievable.

I stare down at her as the waves of pleasure keep passing through her gorgeous body. She's coated in a light layer of sweat. Locks of hair stick to her face. It's the most beautiful thing I've ever seen.

My chest is about to explode with so many emotions I can't identify. I guess that's what love is, when you let it take over.

I caress the side of her face. Gently. Slowly. All the while, waiting for her breaths to calm, even if I'm still panting for air myself.

My thumb finds her bottom lip and I pull at it softly, marveling at how it springs back into place when I let go. So full. So perfect. Perfectly mine.

It takes a minute for both of our bodies to calm. She opens her eyes and looks up at me with a radiant smile on her face.

Thank God, of all the things I see in her, regret

isn't one of them. I could stare at her forever without tiring. My love. My Jill.

"In the cab home that night, when I talked about becoming friends with benefits," she whispers. "I'm so sorry. I was being a fucking idiot."

Her statement takes me by surprise. Then I realize that we might have done something we never have before, but she's still the same person. She's still the same old Jill, who doesn't have much of a filter when she talks. Who shares herself with me. Her doubts, her worries, her frustrations… And right now, her regrets.

"That was rather unexpected," I say.

"It was stupid. I didn't want that. I want so much more. But it came out all wrong, and afterwards I thought I'd ruined our friendship forever. I should have just been honest. With you as well as myself."

I can't express how her words affect me. I'm filled with a warmth I've never felt before. It makes me laugh like she does. With the worst possible timing.

"Honesty is hard."

"Yeah."

I take a deep breath, close my eyes, and remember all the stuff *I* might need to be honest about. Her candor gives me courage for a confession of my own. Although she's invited me to share my deeper thoughts with her in the past, I've always had to hold back because of this great big secret I was hiding.

Well, I'm out now. Why not release the *whole* truth?

"I was hiding in the bathroom earlier, to… you know. Relieve some tension," I say.

Jill tenses, and her eyes widen. "Oh my God! And I interrupted?"

I shrug. "Kinda… I mean… TMI?"

"No wonder you were all grumpy when you came out," she teases.

"It wasn't going particularly well, anyway. Not a big loss in hindsight," I remark.

She presses her lips together tightly, but soon a grin breaks through. "Yeah, I suppose it all worked out in the end."

"Yup." I stare into her eyes for a moment. It did, didn't it? I still can't believe it.

They say 'be careful what you wish for'… This weekend really didn't turn out the way I thought it would. Only a few days ago, I had this expectation that my date with Heather would turn out great, and by the weekend, we might become a real couple.

And now… I have never been more grateful to be dumped on the first date. Again. What a strange realization to have while lying here, literally still inside of the woman of my dreams.

"Damien," Jill says.

"Yeah?"

"I'm sorry I didn't tell you sooner."

"It's okay," I say.

She shakes her head. "No, it's not. My ignorance has been the cause for years of heartache."

Her eyes glaze over a little as she continues to gaze into mine. It's beautiful, the connection we share now. The way we seem to feel what the other is feeling. I have no more use for words right now. Even if all I get to do for the rest of my life is just hold her and look into her eyes like this, that's enough for   me.

CHAPTER FOURTEEN

* Jill *

I don't know how long we've been lying here. With me on my back and Damien still on top of me. *In* me, sort of, though by now things have started to slip out of place.

Despite how quickly everything happened, it really isn't awkward anymore. It's familiar. Safe.

It blows my mind that only two weeks ago I doubted whether the familiar could ever be sexy. I wondered if I needed more mystery than this to get my juices flowing, when really, I never did. I just needed for both of us to be on the same page, and the fireworks would happen all by themselves.

Because the simple fact that I know Damien so well already hasn't ruined the sex. Far from it. It's only made it better. I don't have to pretend, I don't have to act sexy or coy or anything like that. I can just be *me*. And I can tell him *anything*.

Never before have I felt so connected to another human being. Never have I felt so understood and loved.

That's what Damien is to me and always has been, really. My rock. My everything.

I keep touching him, almost by compulsion. His neck. His hair. His face.

I run my hands up and down his back, and over his shoulders. They're so broad, they could carry the world.

As much as we have already confessed, there is still more to say. In two years prior to this moment, we've never run out of things to talk about, and we're not about to now. *We* haven't changed. Only our understanding of our relationship has. And that's beautiful.

"I meant what I told you, earlier," I say, staring up into his pale blue eyes.

I never realized before just how deep they are, like a crystal sea. How much emotion they could contain.

"Hm?"

"I love you," I say, unable to stop smiling. The way he's looking at me, combined with the absolute insanity of being able to say those words to someone and mean them 100% is so overwhelming, I just have to do it again. "I love you!" I squeal.

His expression softens, but he never breaks eye contact.

"I love *you*," he whispers.

"I know!" I grin. God, I know. He's loved me all along. No wonder I always felt so happy around him. I could sense it whenever we were together. I can feel it right now!

In his touch. I see it in his eyes. I know it in the way my chest threatens to explode just from looking at him.

"Never in a million years did I picture this," Damien remarks, a crooked smile playing on his lips.

"No?" I've been picturing this fairly regularly in my dreams.

"I always thought there would be another Frank one day."

I frown. "How do you mean, another *Frank*?" Does he mean another guy?

He smiles briefly. "You know. Another hot, muscular pretty boy."

I shake my head and smile back at him.

"Considering I'm not your type at all," Damien adds.

"You thought *that* was my type?"

"Isn't it? A guy who looks more like Chris Hemsworth, not like… well, me," he explains. "Since he's your celebrity crush and all."

I press my lips together and try not to giggle. My habit of laughing whenever I get tense or nervous has gotten me in enough trouble already tonight.

"I like him as Thor, that's all," I explain.

"Yeah, that's my point. I'm not anything like Thor, and yet, here we are…"

"Oh, but you are, in some ways!" I counter.

He frowns and stares at me in silence.

"I like his character, because although he starts off arrogant and entitled, he's also good-natured.

Trusting. Kind. Generous. And very funny. I love how he always falls for Loki's shit. Not because he's naive, but because he wants to believe that people are essentially good and everyone deserves a second chance."

Kind of like how Damien gave Heather a second chance. And from the sounds of it, a third one. I don't say that, though, quickly adding: "Plus, the romantic storyline with Jane starts off so cute."

"And the physical aspect of his character is what? Irrelevant?" Damien teases.

I shrug. "That's Hollywood for you. It's fake. In fact, I loved how he'd changed in *Endgame*. He wasn't a god anymore, just a regular guy who'd been through some shit."

Damien smiles and shakes his head. "You, Jill, are a weird one."

I shrug and grin back at him. How ironic. These are the types of conversations we used to have before all the bullshit of the past couple of weeks. Just two geeks hanging out and talking about superhero movies. But with one notable exception: we did just have beautifully filthy unprotected sex. Something I would have *never* done if I didn't trust Damien completely. And if I wasn't on the pill.

Actually, now that my body has calmed right down, I want to do it all over again. I think he can tell from the look in my eye, because his expression changes too. The glint in his eye becomes more intense when I wet my lips after glancing up at his.

I make the first move this time. Slowly but surely, tugging at the hem of his t-shirt, I pull it up over his back and finally his head, until his naked torso comes into view. After the conversation we've just had, he might assume I'm not a visual person when it comes to sex, and he'd be wrong. He's been wrong about a bunch of things, but I can't fault him for that.

Taking one glance down at where his chest presses up against mine, I'm done for. I love that he's a bit hairy. It's super hot. I can't stop myself from touching him. Caressing him. Squeezing little bits of him and getting so giddy and excited as a result that my heart might just explode.

"You're way sexier than Thor," I growl, grabbing the back of his neck firmly and pulling him down for a kiss.

"Not possible," he whispers, just as our lips touch.

"I'll prove it to you."

He pulls away again, staring down at my mouth. "Oh yeah, how?"

"Get onto your back and I'll show you!" I boast.

* Damien *

One thing is for sure, I really hadn't pictured *this*. Not even when I let my fantasies run rampant did I allow myself to dream this big.

No sooner has Jill almost ripped my t-shirt off, do I realize the full extent of what's happening. I was ready to be embarrassed. I was ready to feel inadequate in front of her, but she didn't give me a chance to.

Instead, she looks at me like *she's* been starving for years and the only thing to satisfy her hunger is… me. I roll off her and onto my back, and she follows without pause or hesitation.

She devours me with her eyes, and then she devours me with kisses. For the first time ever, I feel like I'm the prize, not her. I'd have to be, for a girl like Jill to react to me this way.

All these years I simply accepted that I didn't deserve her. I never even questioned it. But the way she's worshipping my body now is giving me a whole new understanding of myself and us.

Where I might have doubted myself, she certainly doesn't. She's going to town on me. With her mouth; her hands; her entire body, as she climbs on top, rubbing, tasting, licking, biting…Somewhere along the way she discards her clothes as well, so I can feel the swell of her full breasts brush against me as she moves above me.

She impatiently tugs my shorts all the way off my hips to even the playing field. I finished barely twenty minutes ago, but when she grabs my cock with her right hand, wrapping her fingers around my length and squeezing down hard…

It takes my breath away all over again. I realize that maybe, just maybe, I never went entirely soft. My body knew that that earlier experience was just an appetizer, but the main course was yet to come.

I look down at her and see her face bent low to my groin, her soft lips glistening with saliva, her eyes filled with desire. When she glances up at me, I detect something else in her gaze beyond the obvious lust. There's love there. Affection.

Words evade me, and so I can only watch and feel what comes next. She leans down further, leaning on me with one hand against my thigh. When she takes me into her mouth, my mind goes completely blank. Her lips, so hot and wet; *I can't…*

Instinctively, I flinch, but her hand, travelling up my stomach and resting on my chest, convinces me to relax and enjoy it. She wants this, I remind myself. I didn't ask for it; *she* wants to do it.

Who am I to refuse? No one; that's who.

I am whoever she wants me to be. Her best friend. Her lover. Her humble servant. Her man. And if she wants to honor me like this, then I'll be damned if I'm going to stop her.

So, I try my best to breathe while she starts to move up and down my shaft, sucking me off with a level of confidence and skill I would have never attributed to her even in my wildest fantasies.

But I understand it. It's why I didn't chicken out earlier when she invited me inside her body. Because she trusts me. Completely. Unconditionally. And I trust her.

I realize now that maybe those two years I spent in the friend zone were necessary. Because without them we would have never achieved this level of depth and understanding.

Now that I've shown her my heart, and she showed me mine, I can truly say that I know her. And she knows me. I've never felt more accepted.

As her movements speed up on me, and my cock grows more solid and impatient, fear and doubt no longer have any place in my heart.

She bobs her head up and down my cock, making best use of her whole mouth on me. I feel like my senses are slowly being overwhelmed, and I know that the end is coming. Only then, it doesn't quite happen yet.

She abruptly pulls away just before the moment of reckoning. I open my eyes wide in surprise, but am reassured by the look in hers as she spreads wide and lowers herself down on me. So *this* is what she was after. She wanted to show me to the edge of sanity, only to momentarily reel me back in. It almost backfires, because I'm so close, I can barely stop myself from unloading into her for the second time tonight.

She smiles down at me as she starts to move, overwhelming my senses yet again. God, it feels so good. The heat of her body surrounds me and grips me tightly, and I'm in heaven.

"Touch me," she whispers.

I try. Jesus Christ. I try so hard. One of my hands finds her chest, weighing her breast in my palm and thumbing her rock hard nipple. The other lands on her thigh, before travelling up and back to grab a handful of her toned ass.

Is this really all mine to play with? Am I really allowed to do whatever I want?

Her eyes tell me: yes.

And then her movements speed up, grinding down on me, impaling herself on my cock as deep as it will go. Again and again. Rocking her hips into me. She pries my hand off her hip and places it on her lower abdomen with my thumb facing downward. I understand what she wants, I just don't know how to muster the dexterity to do it properly.

It doesn't matter. Once my thumb rests against her clit, she starts to whimper uncontrollably, all the while keeping up with the insane pace she's set.

She's letting go completely. Going all out. I'm just a passenger on her feverish quest towards the ultimate release.

And as I watch her fall apart on top of me, I can't

stop the tears from welling up in the corner of my eyes. Swept up in the beauty of the moment. Filled with pride that yet again, I was good enough for her. Good enough to please her.

She presses my hand down harder on her mound, and I instinctively wiggle my thumb against the hard nub in between her warm folds. Faster and faster. She shudders and trembles all over.

My balls start to tighten in preparation for what's to come. It takes every ounce of strength I have left to time myself. She cries out my name and grinds to a halt on top of me. That's when I see tears streaming down her face and I know. She's done. As am I.

I buck up into her only once. That's all I need to join her in this moment of beauty.

Our bodies, joined as one yet again, find peace together for the second time tonight. While I watch her catch her breath and fail, I know that this won't be the last time. Not by far.

By the time our alarm goes off in a few hours, we will have done this over and over again. It's been years since I've first wanted to. Finally, we get to make up for lost time.

EPILOGUE

* Jill *

One Month Later.

Things moved pretty quickly once we came back from Glasgow. With a renewed understanding of our relationship, Damien and I worked tirelessly to make our lives fit the new situation.

Neither of us could bear to be apart any longer than we absolutely had to, so we immediately moved in together. We even bought some new furniture to make the place our own, something that I'd been neglecting earlier. Now, I'm glad that I did.

We started shooting *Sealed with a Kiss* barely a week after our return, so we spend our entire days together on set, only to retire to our combined home after hours. And we've never been happier. At least I haven't.

Surprisingly, this new project has had a profound effect on both of our careers. More than I thought it would. Claire had given me a lot of autonomy already, and after Gavin saw the footage from the auditions, he seemed impressed by Damien's work as well. So, we're no longer the inexperienced newbies on set, but instead full members of the senior production team. It's a huge step up.

In what I consider a miracle, Claire managed to secure some extra funding, and as a result, she hired that intern she'd been talking about after all, which freed me up to focus more on operational and creative work. Ours is still a tiny crew, but that has its own perks. Because we're a proper team. All of us, with our own roles to play.

It's been a whirlwind of activity, and by now we're mostly done recording. Five out of the total of six episodes have been wrapped up and moved into post-production. There's one notable exception, which we've tried shooting twice already, to no avail.

Daniel's episode. He was by far my favorite applicant from our little trip to Glasgow, and Owen's as well, once he reviewed the footage.

As Damien predicted, Claire wasn't keen on him as a contestant, but Owen put his foot down. At the time I was glad that he did. But now, it looks like that one decision is about to blow up in everyone's faces.

Because no matter how perfectly matched the female contestants have looked on paper, Daniel's two dates so far have turned into complete disasters. Through no fault of his, I might add. He's been nervous, sure, but he didn't make any of the fatal mistakes you sometimes see guys make on a first date. He isn't self-absorbed. Doesn't come across as a creep. Is an amazing listener and seems to be a nice guy all-round.

As such, things should have gone a lot better for him… Only, they didn't.

And it will put a damper on the entire series if we let him down. To make a feel-good show, we have to secure a happy ending for *him*, more than anyone else. Or do we really want to send the message that someone who has turned his life around against all the odds can't find love, even with the power of science as well as a big television network behind him?

I'm not ready to do that, and neither is Owen nor anyone else on the crew, not even Claire.

It's just a TV show, but we've all become invested in the contestants' lives. And if our viewers feel even half as involved as we do right now, this show is going to take off massively. And then? Who knows. A second season? A third? I secretly hope so, because this is exactly the kind of reality TV I love to watch in my downtime. To be involved in the making of it is a dream come true.

But only if we can give Daniel the romantic success he deserves.

It's late on a Wednesday afternoon when we're called in for a meeting at Claire's office to figure this thing out. When Damien and I arrive, hand-in-hand, Owen and Claire are already waiting for us. Claire smiles briefly when she spots us. I guess she feels smug about being right about our relationship, sort of. Even though at the time there was nothing going on yet.

We take a seat on the small sofa. Right next to each other this time. I love how our legs end up pressed together in the cramped space. Bye-bye, awkwardness! Now, it just feels *nice* to be this close. Comforting.

"Okay, so things haven't gone too well with Daniel so far. What do we do now?" Claire starts. No niceties; no '*hello*'. As usual, she wastes no time before getting to the point.

Damien glances at me in a way that means: 'I told you so.' He didn't like the idea of getting Daniel on as a contestant right from the start. I thought it was jealousy, but perhaps he had an instinct the rest of us didn't.

Owen sits back in his chair and sighs. "Well, this is turning out to be more of a challenge than I thought. The previous matches were near perfect."

"I wonder if everyone was being truthful when they filled out your questionnaire," I comment.

"People have a certain expectation when they come on a reality show like ours. The unwritten rule is that everyone looks like a model, and Daniel definitely does not," Claire says. "But ask whether physical attraction is their number one criterion on a first date, and they'll never admit it."

"He's a great guy, though. I truly believe that he has a lot to offer in a relationship. With the right partner," I add.

Owen nods.

Damien shoots me another strange look. I raise my arms up in silent defense and smile. It's true, though. That's what I believe. His expression softens the longer I look him in the eye. He knows he has nothing to worry about. I'm not about to run off with Daniel, or anyone else for that matter. We're a team. Best friends. Soul mates. Forever. I wouldn't have it any other way.

A loaded silence fills the small room, until Damien breaks it.

"Fake it," he suggests.

All heads turn in his direction.

"That kind of goes against the whole idea of the show," Owen counters. "It would be unethical."

"I don't mean script the entire date or anything like that. Just widen your search a little beyond the regular pool of applicants. Bring in someone who you think will respond well to Daniel. Someone we control who can be sold on Daniel beforehand."

I catch myself staring at Damien. He's so cute when he's being serious. Even if what he's suggesting is a little disingenuous.

"Viewers will be able to tell," Claire interjects.

"The audience isn't stupid."

"Oh, I don't mean an actress or anything. Just a regular person. Set them up like you would a couple of friends, just build the guy up a little when you talk to her before the date. So she knows what to expect."

"Daniel will not respond well to that," Owen says.

"Oh, you mustn't tell Daniel!" I jump in. "He should never find out. It has to feel like a proper blind date to him, or he'll bail!"

Claire sighs and folds her hands behind her head while staring off in the distance.

"Actually, it would be even better if the woman in question doesn't have any aspirations of being on TV. That might have been the problem so far. People lying on the questionnaires because they're hiding that they're really after fame, and not the date itself," I add.

Owen's eyes light up a little and he nods.

Damien and I might both have degrees in Film & TV Production, and not Psychology, but it seems like we're onto something. The only problem is, how do we find this perfect person, who doesn't even want to be on TV, and convince them to participate anyway?

We're all lost in thought, trying to work through the logistics of Damien's idea. Claire is the first to speak up again.

"I might know someone," she says.

Now, all heads turn towards her.

"Oh?" I say.

She nods slowly. "I'm going to need to make a phone call before I'll know for sure."

"I'm not sure I like this," Owen remarks.

"Do we have any other choice?" I ask.

"We're quickly burning through our budget, so we can't keep flogging the same dead horse. We need a sure win. If we try it your way again—" Claire turns to Owen," and it doesn't work out, then we can't even redo the episode anymore, because we'll be out of time and money. In which case your favorite contestant is going to end up alone at the end of our first season, or we're an episode short. And nobody wants *that*, right?" she asks.

Owen shakes his head. "No, definitely not."

"It's worth a try then," I say.

Damien just sits there with a subtle smile playing on his lips. Troubleshooting isn't even his job, technically. But he's still pretty good at it. Who would have thought? Oh yeah, me! In my opinion, he can do anything.

I can't stop staring at him. Funny how I see him so differently now. He's unmistakably still the same guy I've been friends with for years. Exactly the same.

But ever since I realized my true feelings, he almost looks different. More handsome than before. Incredibly sexy. Perfect in every way.

Guess that's what happens when you have your

rose-tinted glasses on.

I block the side of my face with my hand so Claire and Owen don't see what I'm about to do.

"I love you," I mouth at Damien.

His eyes are already locked onto mine as if I'm the only thing in the whole world that matters to him. I know what this stare means. It means he loves me too.

It also means that as soon as we're done with this meeting and at home, he's going to *show me*.

On my back. Underneath me. With his face between my thighs. He's going to show me how he feels about me, in every possible way.

And I'll be insatiable. Because to be on the receiving end of his affections is something I can never get enough of. It's why I used to seek him out all the time even before we became a couple. Why I used to love it every time I'd catch him looking at me on set.

Love makes the world go 'round. And the fact that I found it with my best friend makes me the luckiest girl on earth.

With a bit of luck, Damien's idea will work out and Daniel—along with our tiny little show—can have a happy ending of his own. Everyone's circumstances and journeys are different, but love, companionship… *family;* those   are   things *everyone* deserves.

Life's too precious to have to spend it alone.

AUTHOR'S NOTE

Thanks so much for reading *Best Friends Forever*.

Perhaps you've been following me for a while, perhaps you're new to my work. But now that you're here, I'd like to give you a little background on how this book came to be...

My writing career started all the way back in October 2012 when I took a very deep breath, closed my eyes, crossed my fingers and even my toes and clicked 'Publish' on my first short story. That steamy little piece called *Ladies' Day*, and the book it grew into eventually ([Beautiful Stranger](#)) are still relevant today because it features a curvy heroine and her older lover. It serves as my first foray into steamy body positive romance.

Since then, I've published a whole bunch of other books, in various romance sub genres; as L. Moone I write contemporary, and as Lorelei Moone I write about shifters, vampires and other paranormals. Certain themes tend to repeat themselves throughout my catalogue.

Beauty lies in the eye of the beholder. The hang-ups we tend to have about ourselves and our bodies often aren't shared by the opposite sex. While it's a lot more popular to write about gorgeous curvy ladies and their athletic admirers than the other way around, but I've dabbled in both in the past. I just never felt there was a big market for husky men in romance. 2020 changed that thanks to the likes of Jessa Kane and her sexy big boy titles, *Hefty* and *Husky* (she published a few more similar titles by now). I'm slowly seeing other authors enter this space, so perhaps the time has come? I hope so, because I'd love to write a whole bunch more of these...

While the body positive aspect of *Best Friends Forever* comfortably fits into the rest of my catalogue, it's also a bit different. It's a friends-to-lovers romance; my first ever one! Thinking back, I'm not quite sure why I've never written one before, because my real life relationship with my husband totally started that way.

When I first met my husband, I was still involved with another guy, but we hit it off immediately. Here was someone who had a similar sense of humor, a bunch of shared interests, and whom I could talk to for hours. Just as a friend. As we got closer, people around us started to get suspicious and wondered if something else was going on, but we were both completely oblivious to it. We were just really good friends! Except...

My existing relationships was on its last legs, and I confided in my now-husband. We talked about everything. His past relationships. My current one. The fact that I was in a foreign country (I had emigrated to be with my ex), and considering moving back home after breaking up with him... When suddenly, something happened. An accidental touch. A funny reaction, butterflies, desire, infatuation; all the stuff we never thought would happen as a result of that single moment of physical contact. A sudden shift in perspective which meant that we went from being completely platonic to crazy passionate about each other in a single night. Within days we decided that this was it; we were going to be together forever. So, as you might imagine, I've had a lot of real-life inspiration to draw from for *Best Friends Forever*.

There's something very interesting to me about already knowing your significant other very well before ever getting involved romantically. You kind of skip the initial awkwardness of being attracted to someone while not really knowing what makes them tick yet.

It can be messy as well, though. Especially when one person is already in love, and the other has no idea. Unrequited love is so painful, and makes a person behave in very strange ways. These are the situations and themes I tried to explore in this book.

Anyway, this book is also a continuation of the work I've done earlier this year in *Recipe for Passion (Husky Men Do It Better Book 1)*; it's me doubling down on the big man romance trend (Is it a trend yet? It should be; let's make it one!) So, if you enjoyed *Best Friends Forever* and you haven't read *Recipe for Passion* yet, I hope you'll check that out too.

I'm already working on the next installment in the *Big Boys Do It Better* series but it might take me a couple of months, so in the meantime I would like to point you to some other Big Boy books in my catalogue: Just Another Day at the Office and One Night Stand.

And that's enough from me. I hope you enjoyed the story as much as I did while writing it, and if you're interested in reading more of my work, perhaps you'll consider signing up for my newsletter. I'll even give you a free short story when you sign up.

x, Lorelei

FIND ME AT:

LMoone.com
Lorelei Moone on Facebook
AuthorLMoone on Instagram

I also write Paranormal Romance as Lorelei Moone. Check out LoreleiMoone.com for more information.

SPECIAL OFFER!

For a limited time, all new mailing list subscribers will receive a FREE short story, called At First Sight.

Claim your free copy here:

LMoone.com

Look for the newsletter sign-up form at the bottom of the page.

YOUR NEXT READ?

Recipe for Passion isn't the only big boy romance book I've written over the years.

It's actually the start of a new series, called Big Boys Do It Better, which is going to release throughout 2021.

But until then, do check out the following titles:

JUST ANOTHER DAY AT THE OFFICE

Bloody typical. Day one at the new job, and I'm crushing so hard on my colleague I can't think straight.

John isn't your average romance novel hero. He doesn't have a way with the ladies, neither does he have six pack abs. He's just a regular guy with a bit of a dad bod, and he's shy and awkward rather than suave and charming.

That's cool, because I'm just a regular girl. One who's already head over heels for him and he doesn't even realise it...

Available to order from all major book retailers - ISBN: 9781913930028

I was only looking for Mr. Right Now...

All I want is a night of distractions to take my mind off the stressful business meetings I've had day. At the pub, I quickly spot the perfect counterpart to share tonight with. Whereas I'm all business, he's tall, burly, long-haired as well as tattooed. We're nothing alike, and yet click almost immediately.

Could it be that I have accidentally stumbled across Mr. Right?

Available to order from all major book retailers - ISBN: 9781913930080

OTHER PUBLICATIONS

THE CHANCE ENCOUNTERS SERIES:

One Night Stand (A Big Boy Romance)
Paperback ISBN: 9781913930080
Beautiful Stranger (A Curvy Girl Romance)
Paperback ISBN: 9781913930103
Only a Taste (A Curvy Girl Romance)
Paperback ISBN: 9781913930127
Chance Encounters: The Collection
Paperback ISBN: 9781913930141

THE UNDATEABLES SERIES:

The Rebound List (A Steamy Chicklit Novel)
Paperback ISBN: 9781913930042
Sally (A Steamy Chicklit Novella)
Paperback ISBN: 9781913930066
Undateables: The Collection
Paperback ISBN: 9781913930158